I0671517

GLAMMARIS©

THOT LIFE

CRESHIE WRITES©

GLAMMARIS THOT LIFE©
Copyright © 2015 by Creshie Writes

All rights reserved. No part of this book may be reproduced or transmitted in any form or by any means without written permission from the author.

Printed in USA by Create space
Cover graphic design by the amazing Patrick

Thank you...

To my heavenly father for making life possible to live. To my family, friends and Sistahs' for their support. Special shout out to my chapter by chapter readers, Monica, Tia, Shameek, and Velera. Thank you for pushing page after page out of me. Last but not least special thanks to Onika Maraj for the advice to "To never be afraid to push my pen."

"Thot life is a lifestyle of living every moment thru a unforgettable sex-pereience"

-Glammaris

#thotyhottyonfleek!

Yes, I'm Glammaris, a B A D bitch, boobies, ass and dollars, and I know you've heard, I'm a hoe, side chick, smut and or a thot but I'm gonna tell you the truth and shatter all the myths involving my name. What they didn't tell you was I am 120 pound honey dipped, pretty face, chinky eyes, thin waist, fat ass with a sick weave rolling on red heels. Yes I fuck and suck for buck and don't give a fuck. No I'm not on the street corner selling ass and mouth. I select the men or niccas that I charge for sex. Females are so quick to look down on me but in all actuality we all do the same thing in different ways. I'll show you. Okay you living with your baby father, man, boo thing or whatever you want to call him and he is paying the rent, right? Stop fucking him and see it he still pay your rent. So the reality of it basically breaks down to you fucking him to pay your rent. Or you kicking it with a nicca and he gets you gear, kicks, hair and nails done. He just tipping you for sex you already gave him. It's not what you do but how you do it. See what makes me different is I fuck different niccas for my rent money. So my rent is paid 6 times by 6 different men or niccas in 1 month. And I don't fuck for tips I gotta be paid up front.

Chicks hate on me cause they wish they could look as good as I do, doing what I do. Ya heard. How many times have you heard a female or yourself has said *"He can get it"* but never go get that dick? Well I'm a go getter! Niccas can't knock the hustle so most of my friends are niccas. It's the beginning of the summer. The summer is real good money, if you know whatcha doing. I turn heads all day in winter gear but I make nicca's eyes drool in the summer dresses. A nicca will steal from his own mama to get between these legs. I have already dropped the dead weight from last winter. I had exhausted their pockets and no longer had the drive to fuck them. Right now I have the same 2 ride or dies from back in the date. 1st there's Louie. Louie has a full time job, a wife and 4 kids. That leaves zero time for me and that added up great in my pockets. He was basically paying me to stop by the garage where he works so his co-workers would think he was fucking me. I am a good look for him. Shit I played right along with his grease monkey ass. I'll doll up and walk in there all eyes were on me with their mouths open. Mind you, we never hugged or kissed upon greeting each other ever but "people" read deep into nothing. The "people" is the spectators and speculators that don't know about me personally but know everything personal about me. In my presence all Louie's co-workers stared with lust dripping from their pores like the grease dripping from their uniform jumpsuits. But behind my back their jealousy was screamed I was "fucking" grease monkey Louie for his money. Well let's face it, I only talked to his 52 year old ass for the money but fucking him was absolutely out of the question, yes, even for me. I had to say that. People get it twisted all the time, just 'cus I get paid for my services, I'm outchere sucking and fucking every men or nicca moving. There's levels and rules to my life style that can change at any molly moment LOL! But fucking grease monkey Louie was absolutely out of the question. 6 years strong with no physical contact between myself and the grease monkey and I was rewarded with a weekly pay of 2 hundred to 3 hundred dollars. And I stop by twice a week. Once maybe on a Tuesday or on a Wednesday to make sure we good for Friday and then on Friday to pick up my funds. Then there's Gabriel. Me and Gabe grew up together. We have on and off relationship since 2nd grade. Gabe was always trying to save me and I was trying to save him but neither one of us needed to be saved. Gabe was content with being the average nicca with a 9 to 5, living life by the rules. I was trying to rescue him from boredom and he was trying to cage my sexual liberation. He didn't have an adventurous side like me. Gabe talked a good one but he couldn't provide me with the things I wanted. I think he felt guilty for taking my virginity, he act like he failed me in some way. Who know I would fall in love with fucking? I've explained it to him 100 times, my life is livable. Shit what female have you seen walking thru the hood with an official assorted Gucci on their shoulder? Or seen a female rocking Alexander McQueen with the latest on their feets? From heel to sneaker? Who has the best of best premium weave, a band per bundle? With their nails stuck on fleek? Gabe's famous line "But look how you got it?" So does it cost less cause I fucked or sucked for the money? I don't think so. If anything it should cost more. Sorry I got distracted by my phone ringing. Why niccas don't respect the curve? This nicca Monty is a straight sucker for love ass nicca. He has his BM, 2 kids and they all live under the same roof but he claims to want to be with me. I ain't the want to be with type of gurl and he knew this before the 1st stroke. LML! From my line of work I have come up with the conclusion every man is a shark and can't be trusted. Men are the original hoes! LOL! Okay I'll start from the beginning and give you the drop on Monty's pitiful ass. Monty use to come by the club every Friday night and make it shower 200 dollars in ones for like a month. Then one day I was going home from my morning jog. Yes I run and I also have a fitness training every Monday afternoon. I gotta keep this ass sitting up right with a small waist, how else I going to make my money. Shit don't nobody do shit for me. I've been on my own since moms cut off support, I was 16 years old when that happened. I moved out of my mom's apartment at 18 with a high school diploma. And I've been living by myself ever since with no handouts. That means I have been take care of myself for a long fucking time now. Well any way I ran right in Monty like 5 blocks from my apartment. We were both staring at each other but couldn't figure out where we know each other from. It clicked in my head before his mind solved the puzzled look on his face. I was ready to part ways with his sexy ass, but he was lingering around for more

Wednesday, June, 28th

conversation, inviting me into a coffee shop for a cup of coffee. I usually don't acquaint or fuck niccas I meet at work. Think about it, when a men or nicca pay his cover charge to a strip club he is looking for free tities and ass, period. So every time they see me they are thinking free tities and ass. And there's nothing free about the way I talk or walk. Monty was square and I would've enjoy playing square for a little while with him. He is about 6 feet, solid. Sexy lips on his creamy milk chocolate skin. By all means Monty is definitely eye candy for the women, MCM for the ladies and of course taken, I noticed the wedding band on his manicured finger. He was nicely groomed, definitely a metrosexual. So at this point we have exchange conversation. He articulate very well. I was completely turned on by the way he spoke about his wife and kids. He spoke with admiration and pride for his family. I'll let y'all in on a secret, men can only cheat when things are good with their girl slash wife. When a man is fighting with his mate, he is unable to cheat cause his mate is all he is thinking about. I just wanted to fuck him 2 good times. I say 2 times cause the way my pussy is set up, all new dick feel good and if it don't I'm generous enough to give a 2nd chance to fuck this pussy right. LML! Fucking Monty was the closest I would ever come to his lifestyle. His eyes brighten with words of his home and job. But there was a fog of sexual tension hanging over us. For all the sex I've sold I could give just one freebie, right? So I did. And I tell no lies the shit was the best sex I've had in a minute, literally breath taking. See the niccas and men I fuck with are trying to get their money's worth or I'm just trying to get one off. LOL! But with Monty it was pure desire. We went to my apartment, which is a no no, but I was completely mesmerized by his mannerisms. Before my apartment door could closed behind him, I attacked. I pulled his V-neck tee shirt over his milk chocolate baldhead. Seeing his muscular chest and six pack abs in the nude excited my sexual senses. He switched roles and became the aggressor. He lift me up and sat me on the kitchen's marble counter top. He was wrestling with my leggings. I kicked my running sneakers off and assisted with the leggings and my underwear. He pulled my ass close to the edge of counter top. He wasted no time he inhaled my clit with his milk chocolate pillow soft lips. My head drop back from the instant satisfaction. He released my clit and slowly but firmly massage my pussy with his warm long tongue. He inserted his tongue into my pussy. He then glide his tongue from my pussy to my asshole and then back to my pussy. When he came up for air my cream was dripping from his goatee. My juices dripping from his lips and hairs on his chin made me cum. He unbuckled his belt and slacks, slipped into a condom. Then he filled my pussy with his penis. His strokes were steady and firm. The lustful kisses to my neck down to nipples made me thrust my pussy on to his penis with force. As the strokes intensify so did the hugging of his arms around my ribs. His hands had a firm grip on my fat ass. The strokes changed from fast to rapid along with his breathing. He then lifted me up off of the counter top and laid me on the bare floor. He introduced my face to knees by raising my legs above my head. His penis never being freed from the closing in of my pussy's walls. He stood over me like a muscular milk chocolate giant. I was completely wrapped up in the moment. We fucked that entire day all over my apartment. And I was willing to walk away and accepted the sex-perience for what it was, the heat of the moment. Now mind you I lived in my apartment for 3 years and never ran into him before that day. But after our heated session I was bumping into him at least twice a week and seeing him every Friday night at the club. He was practically looking and lurking for another fuck. At 1st Monty was concerned a black man now I see him as a whining bitch nicca. A black man fights against the walls of box that was built for him. A black man lives up to what society considers a "model citizen" while handling his own responsibilities. A nicca is one who has accepted and is content with living according to stereotypic walls, never looking to expand his horizon, never developing to full potential outside the box. Anybody can be a nicca, but not every man can be a black man. Monty has reduced himself to a common irritating nicca. I straight up ignored him on every sighting. He had even lost the respect I would give to a low level nicca. Its soooo quiet for him!!Lesson learned never give away charity pussy cause niccas can't accept a fucking gift and I thought females were supposed to be the emotional ones. I'm here to tell you niccas are quick to turn emotional and stalker-ish off of one fuck faster than women. I didn't want Tank to tune his ass down but he was kinda like forcing my hand. I told Monty to fuck me again it will cost him a band to hold him off for a minute. With a wife, kids and responsibilities it should take him a year to be able to spurge a $1,000. Tank is my Bro, not by blood. We met like 4 years ago. Yeah we fucked, one good time. We have love for each other like brothers and sisters except for the sex part. Sex with tank was like a long love song, without words. The extreme sexual humidity whenever we shared the same space was too hot for me. It was a turn on to see Tank be hard in these streets and be so gentle in the sheets. His passion in the sheet was like music. A smoothing melody with a strong beat. Tank is a street nicca. He hustled on street corners most of his 25 yrs. of life and he handles all thing by old school street code, the code that was pasted down from his father, to his brother, too him. Tank wasn't your average nicca. He was smooth but deadly. He was extra smart too. He could turn flour into dough overnight, a for real hustler. He took the lessons and money from the street and turned it legit. And just because he thought outside of the project's bricks, I admired and respected Tank. If Monty keep his shit up he will have to deal with Tank's goons. Monty is straight up and down disrespecting the curve.

Like FOH!!! Stalking in person and on my jack. SMFH! I want to know which of them jealous bitches at club give him my number. Them spiteful bitches at work are pure haters. One of them bitches told Black that I was fucking niccas in the private lap dance rooms, when I know every dancer that ever worked up in there has done it at least once. For that right price, I have no problem pulling my G-string to the side and handle my business, if I feel like it! So now I'm being fake watched. FOH. I hate the fucking politics that comes with that club. I work 4 nights a week. Wednesday is the slow day, I take the center stage only once, the rest of the night Black want dancers to walk around try to influence private lap dances. Each time on center stage is $50 in pay. The hourly rate is $4.75 per hour for 20 hours a week and your tips are yours. Private lap dance are on 25% commission per dance, with breakdown to $12.50 per dance on your paycheck. Thursday, Friday and Saturday I clean house. I go on stage 3 times each night and an average of 12 private lap dances per night. So my weekly check from the club is like $700 and some change after taxes. Yes I pay taxes, we even have a health insurance plan, it's a real job.

Which reminds me that I have to get my annual physical, Black goes extra hard for his little medical form. So I get paid little over $700 plus tips and my extra hundreds I pick up along the way, weekly. LOL! The money is great, it's the other shit that comes with it that I don't like. Them so called females that work there are a bunch of cut throat type bitches, they will steal your lap dance right from under your nose. I have the best hours 11pm to 4am and the best days I know them bitches be hating cause every week they fussing with Black "Why does she have a set schedule every week and everybody else days and hours change every week?" but they never once asked or said anything to me. I would've told them the truth, Naturel is on Black's payroll working his dick. Naturel is 4 years older than me. She is my bestie, my sister, when I need. And for the right price my lover, JK! She was currently rooming at my apartment. And them bitches at work would die if they knew Black was paying half of my rent and be throwing me Sundays to work for extra cash. LML!! I laugh at them clown bitches at work. I'm 21 year old I don't plan on being a dancer for the rest of my life. Nor was I waiting on daddy Warbucks to fall in love with me from a lap dance, tight pussy or best head ever and rescue me. Them bitches are washed up and their teeth needed a brush down from all the shit they talk. LMAO!!!! I'm waiting on Naturel to hook me up with a high scale night club gig, the pay is better, human customers not the beast that come to Black's club, and the best part is I get to keep my clothes on. Well its Wednesday and it 9pm, got to get ready for work. But 1st let me post my WCW. I posted Tanya Harding! You gotta respect a boss bitch that would sick a goon to break another bitch leg for what she wants! Whether it's on an ice skating ring or on the street. #SALUTE! BRB!

Thursday, June, 29th

Last night started off wrong... my regular driver Mohammad had called out sick and Nicholas was my driver for the night. That meant I had to pay for my ride. See with Mohammad I could bat my eyes and jerk his dick as payment for my ride to and from the club. With Nicholas I was gonna have to pay. Nicholas was chit chatting about whatever I had blocked him out cause I was annoyed that I really was gonna have to pay. SMFH!! Then once I got to the club I found out that the only time I'm on stage was taken from me and given to Sugar, nasty ass. Black had completely lost his fucking mind. I was heading to his office to confront his black ass when Jah, security, stopped me. You can fight the other dancers, you can even cuss out the deejay but you cannot fuck with security. I repeat, YOU CAN NOT FUCK WITH SECURITY! Security had the power of controlling the niccas inside and outside the club. If I had a problem with security, when a nicca grab my ass or just straight up disrespect me, I'll be on my own. Plus I hated Jah big black ass. See I danced and lived in Brooklyn but Harlem is where I call home, my hood. Harlem bred, born and raised. Jah is from my hood. He told any and every nicca from the hood that I worked at a strip club. I hated him not for telling but for the fact that he felt that he needed to tell people my business which was none of his or their business. As a dancer having beef with Jah is too much of a risk to my safety. He's the type of nicca too see to it that something happens to me. So I backed away from the door and called Naturel. She tells me that, her and Black are fighting cause he was still fucking other females but didn't want her to fuck niccas for money. I wanted to say, well fuck them for free, but she wasn't in a playful mood. LML. I really wanted to snitch Black's ass out and tell her to add Sugar's nasty ass to his list but somethings is better left unsaid. The crazy shit is I'm caught up in the middle of their bullshit. So I worked the hell out of a dead night, I had no choice. But at midnight things started turning up. It was an inspiring rapper's birthday. His record label came up in the club 50 deep, associates were spontaneously arriving it was about 100 men in the grand VIP room. The way the club is set up, there are 2 floors. The 1st floor, has two bars one on the left and one on the right side of the square shaped room. In between the two bars is the "Floor". The floor has 4 mini stages with a pole in the center. Females working the floor is bottom level of employment. Their pay rate is $3.75 per hour. Black be having them dance for two hours before their break and then it's back on the floor for the rest of the night and they only work the weekends. The main stage is at the end of both bars. The entrance to the private lap dance rooms is between the main stage and the ends of the bars. The 2nd floor is VIP. On the right side are 3 mini VIP rooms. On the left side was the grand VIP in the center and one medium size VIP. The rooms on the second floor all had glass walls. Back to last night, you know them thirsty hoes that work there was all on it. Jacking Black to let them work the grand VIP. Black was eating up the attention. I walked right pass the hurdle around Black and went to my locker. The locker room is in the basement of the club. I was changing my outfit I had just given a lap dance and the guy nutted on himself, it came thru his pants on to my ass. I was completely grossed out from the sex-perience. An sex-perience that happened too often. Black walks over to me and announced I'll be one of the few in the grand VIP room. I would've never ask him but he was trying to right his wrong. He know he had no fucking business taking my stage time but the grand VIP is better I guess. While shaking my ass in the indoor rain a guy name Emery asked me to have a sit and have a drink with him. "Your beauty is magnifying." Is what he said. I get compliments all the time but his was genuine. I didn't mind sitting with him, either way I was going to get my commission. 10% of $5000 plus tips. These nicca was in here throwing $100 in the air like 1s. I was clapping this ass encouraging them to blow some more in the air. The more they spent it the fast this ass go. Yeah the night had turned up and around. Well this Emery claims to have night clubs, yes with an "s", in Miami and other places and is hosting a liquor debut party and would like me to represent his club, with accommodations of a free flight to and from and $2,500 in cash per day. I was in but told him I'll think about. I acted as if I get offers like this all the time. He handed me his card and said don't think to long the flight leaves Friday morning. What you think, should I go? When I left the club I was glowing. I had made 4 bands in tips. I was feeling so good that I invited Nicholas white ass to breakfast. We went to a chicken and waffle spot on 133rd and 7th avenue.

Thursday, June, 29th

I found out Nicholas is the heir to the car service company. He father is the owner. He was freely airing his disperses. How his father don't respect or trust him. How his long term girlfriend wants him to get a "real" job. I ate and listen. Then he started showering me with compliments with an undertone of disapproval. "How such a beautiful girl could use her looks to live?" I wanted to tell him my how much I enjoyed doing what I do, when I'm doing it but I didn't want Nicholas all up in my BI. After breakfast Nicholas drop me off at home. It was 6 am. I wanted to take a nap but I had pop a molly before going to club so I was wide awake. Some people get liquid courage from alcohol well I get my sexual freak courage from popping a molly or two. When I'm high of the molly it's like I'm watching myself perform the sexual acts while exploiting every sex-perience in body and mind. I decided to clean up the apartment. Naturel is a bit of a slob. She had the living room looking like a clothes bomb went off. Of course when I was finished Naturel came rolling thru the door. After she showered. She begin telling the story of the argument between her and Black. I was half listening. Females who use their body for profit can't keep no man. And that's just the facts. Men are not comfortable sharing their shit. Let me tell y'all a little story about my other bestie Ivory. Ivory would've been right here chilling with me and Naturel right now. Ivory was living life just like me and Naturel but tried to keep a man. She was working at the club with me. She had a man and respected their relationship. She just dance, she didn't sell sex but a nicca at the club offered her 2 bands for sex. It was an offer she couldn't refuse. Ivory accepted the offer. She planned to use the money to put down on a car for man's birthday as a surprise gift. Ivory was in the hotel room fucking when her man busted in the room and shot her. He shot her in the back while she was riding the dick to buy him a set of wheels. She is now paralyzed from the waist down. She rolls 24 on wheels, not exactly what she asked for. You can't have no man while selling sex. Naturel was still crying, sobbing, and talking about Black's ass. She knew the rules to this. I wanted to but my heart wouldn't let me feel sorry for her not matter how she try to buy my heart. I just couldn't stay in the apartment with the depressing fog inside. I decide to go to my mom's crib. When I entered my mom's crib I immediately started

Thursday, June, 29th

cleaning. That molly had me lit. There was clothes, mickey d's wrappers and toys everywhere, on the coffee table, floor, and on the couches. Once the living room was clean I started cleaning the kitchen. I came across a cute picture of me, Goldie and Gia. Goldie was 12 yrs old, I was 10 yrs and Gia was 8 yrs old in the picture. We stood in age order. We had on ballerina outfits in our favorite colors. Goldie in purple, me in pink and Gia in blue. We were sisters no triplets. I guess my parents didn't get that memo. Me and Goldie are like oil and water. Goldie was a tom boy-ish and I'm girlie. She dug up worms out of dirt when we were young, Eweeee! Gia is the quiet one. I guess our favorite color matched our personalities. The color purple has the ability to appear to be other colors like blue or black, one could forget that it is still purple matching Goldie perfectly. The color pink is commonly equated to bags, bras, lip sticks, nail polish, panties, perfumes and shoes, all the things I love, so hell yeah I match my color. Gia is at peace, it shows in her calm voice tone, just like the color blue is tranquility. Gia had the power of saying a lot without talking. I post the pic on my IG page for TBT. I turned around and Kayla and Taylor was standing in the kitchen doorway staring at me. Kayla is 6 yrs. old and Taylor is 4 yrs. old. They are my little sister and brother. "Where's mommy?" they asked. Shit, I assumed she was in her room. So I went to check. Nope, she wasn't in her room. My moms is something else. How could she leave a 6 and 4 year old kids in the apartment alone? I put them in the tub cause their night clothes looked dusty. I washed and combed Kayla hair which had dirty, lint and was matted to her scalp. I got them dressed in clean fresh clothes and gave Kayla the cuties two ponytails. I photo bombed them and posted their pics on IG. We had to go to the supermarket cause there was no food in the refrigerator. I let them pick out their snacks and cereals. I plan to just get a few things and ending up doing a full food shopping. The bag packer pushed the cart of food to the apartment door, as I lead the way. Jah black ass was in front of the building with a squad of niccas. He had the nerve to say good morning. I keep it pushing. He going to yell out "We should be cool since we work together." I didn't even look back at his simple ass. I hate Jah ass, for real. I sat the kids down in front of the TV to watch cartoon as I made them waffles, eggs and sausage. Finally my moms falls thru the door. I can tell she was drinking. She reeked of a week in a bottle. "Before you say a word I was just downstairs at Smitty's house, they could've came and got me, they know where Smitty lives." I did as she asked and didn't say a word. If I did we would've ending up fighting. I really wanted to punch her face in for leaving my sister and brother alone to fuck Smitty for a few coins. She has been fucking Smitty since I was Kayla's age. My moms took a dry waffle and went to the bathroom. She came to the living room all freshened up. Trying to stuff the kids in their room with sippie cups. The juice was laced with Visine's eye drops cause she was having company. The Visine eye drop would put the kids to sleep for a minimum of 5 hours. I know 1st hand she has drugged me before in my younger days. I went in the room with the kids making sure they didn't drink the tainted juice. We cleaned their room together. My moms's company had arrived and disappeared in to my mom's walls. I took the kids to park in front of the building to play. I didn't want to hear my moms get her back dig in or out and I didn't think my little sister and brother should listen to her moans either. Jah and his squad was still out front. I walked right pass him. He steady trying to have conversation. FOH! He questioning me. "How could I grind on strangers but couldn't speak to him? How could I treat him like he some ugly nicca?" I just stared at him with the "kill yourself" eyes. Earl walked up on the scene and dismissed Jah. Earl is my moms next door neighbor. His occupation is a bike messenger, since he was 14 years old. I don't know if was the fact that he was fighting against the air every day all day that made is eyes jump from the socket or made his bottom lip hang or made his skin gremlin texture but that what he looked like. I tell no lies Earl is one ugly mother fucker. Earl is hard on the eyes but easy on the heart. He is genuinely a good person with a heart sweet as candy. Earl has been coming to my rescue since we were in 5th grade. In 5th grade I had pulled my skirt up for Bobby Valentine's lunch money. Bobby told the whole school and after school boys was chasing me home. It was ugly ass Earl that started laying nicca out for me. Earl chased the thought of me out of their minds. In junior high school I jerked off, gave and got top, from several niccas for different things, clothes, jewelry, and sneakers. I thrived off the fact I got what

Thursday, June, 29th

I wanted without actually fucking. I had to survive the best way I could. At 14years old I give my virginity to Gabe. I went to my moms after the fact. Her 1st question was "Did he cum? Cause if he didn't cum, you ain't doing it right!" she then proceeded to pull out a 9 inch dildo. She stuck the dildo to the wall, it had a suction cup on the end of it. "A man can get pussy anywhere but a good dick sucker is hard to find!" She said as she begin to give step by step instruction along with demonstration of how to suck a dick to her 14 year old daughter. She put the icing on the cake by saying "There be no wet pussies and dry pockets in my house!" Slowly she started buying less and less clothes and sneakers for me. Sooner than later she had completely stop supporting me, it was all about her new man and Kayla growing in her stomach. And in her opinion since I was having sex, my pussy should pay my way. On my junior high school graduation day after the ceremony I post every nicca's name that I sucked his dick or he sucked on my pussy on my myspace page. Bitches and niccas was gunning for my head but Earl held me down. You ask why would I post the list? Cause bitches always had my name on their lips bout who I was fucking or who I already fucked. So I posted the list so there was no more guessing or lying. In high school bitches hated on me from what they had heard, some of it was true and some of it was pure lies. So I only chilled with the niccas. I struggle thru high school my moms was only providing a roof over my head and nothing more. I was fully responsible for feeding and clothing myself. Back to today, after the kids had played in the park for over an hour I took the kids back to my mom's crib. My mom's company had fucked, paid and left. My moms was asking about my life like she gave a fuck. My eyes looked at my moms beautiful face and viewed the ugly things she have done. People, places and things can have the sweetest outside and have a completely sour core. I went next door to Earl's apartment, he was easier to look at right then. Earl was a serious loud head. I smoked with him trying to come down of the molly. Earl could read the look in my eyes. DTF was s-creaming from my eyes and shouting from my pores. Earl would give me the shirt off his back if I wanted it. I won't ever charge Earl for sex cause I fucked Earl out of pleasure. Earl is an ugly mother fucker but he was hung like a horse. See I have this theory, men that were ugly in high school have big dicks. Cause while the pretty niccas was getting all the pussy they was home jerking their dick giving their dicks some extra inches. Goldie say "Big noses" well Earl is an ugly nicca with a big nose. I kicked off my pink glitter Christian Louboutin and hopped on Earl's bed. I unbutton my True Religion jeans and took off my powder pink off the shoulder tee shirt. I wrapped my top of the line weave into a bun and laid back. Earl was nervous. He lit another blunt. I usually would wait for Earl to make the 1st move but the molly had my sexual hormones racing. As Earl smoked I leaned over his back and started massaging the bulge in the front of his pants. He quickly put the blunt down and stood up. He took off all his clothes and I followed his lead. I laid on my back. He grabbed my right foot and begin massaging it. His right thumb was moving in a circular motion on the ball of my foot while his left thumb moved in the same circular motion on the heel of my foot. I was completely unwinding in his hands. He then licked and sucked on my toes then he performed the same technique on my left foot. His tongue on my toes made my pussy wet. He then moved up to my ankles. He massaged the inside of my ankle with his thumb and the outside of my ankle with his index finger. His fingers was calming my muscles as my pussy tightened with desire. He moved up to my calf. He used both hands on my right calf. His fingertips danced up and down my calf as his thumbs massage my shin. My pussy was pulsating with anticipation. The sexual heat was not only building in my pussy but in Earl's dick too. He massaged my left calf the same way. He kissed my kneecaps before he parted my legs. He kneed down to kiss the inside of my thighs, 1st the right side then the left side. He then used his index finger and middle finger to part my pussy's lips open. His tongue danced on my clit while his chin grinded on my pussy's opening. My back bucked every time I came on his chin. He then kissed my stomach. He dragged his tongue up to my right breast. He cupped my breast with his left hand and dragged his tongue up down and across my nipple. He used his index and middle finger to massage my clit. His rigid fingertip on my clit and rough tongue on my nipple made me cum on his right hand's touch. My cum slid down his finger into the palm of his hand. He used his right hand to guide his monster penis into my wet pussy. My body jerked from the sudden mix feelings of pain and pleasure coming over me all at once. He push until the monster penis was deep inside my stomach. The tightness of my pussy's walls caused him to quickly pull the monster penis out in fear of launching off too early. He wanted to savor the moment. He planted kisses on my right nipple. He then guided the monster penis back inside of my wet pussy I jerked again. He slowly glided his monster penis deep into my stomach again. He wrapped his arms around my back. He held me tight as his monster jabs go from slow and steady to fast and wild. His heavy jabs and breathing in my ear was turning me on. I throw my hips in the air to meet the monster's heavy punches. He pulled the monster out of my pussy and gently flipped me onto my stomach. I was laying on my stomach holding my ass up in the air by standing on my knees and elbows. He guided the monster inside my dripping wet pussy as I backed my pussy up on the monster dick. He used his hands to massage my shoulders. He massage down my back using his thumbs to dance down my spine. My body inhaling the pleasure from his hands as my pussy exhaled pleasure indulgence from the pain endurance of his monster. When his hands reached my waist his took to a firm hold on my

Thursday, June, 29th

hips his thumps meeting at the curve in my back and a hail storm of heavy jabs was pounded into my dripping wet pussy. My pumped ass cheek bounced off his stomach with every jab, making a clapping sound. He used his hands to hold my ass cheeks open so he could get the whole monster inside. His jabs punched into a waterfall of coated water. His monster was stomping thru my wet pussy. From the loud moans and pulsating from the monster I could tell after an hour and 22 minutes Earl had finally came. I took a shower got dressed and was ready to call my car service, why Earl begged for me stay til I go to work? But I had shit to do I couldn't just lay up with him. Besides I couldn't look at his ugly ass all damn day. LML! I promised to come see him when I come back from Miami. Yup, I decided to go. So I called my car service. And fucking Nicholas showed up. Shit I got to pay again. I went to the Christian Louboutin store on 76th street and 5th avenue. I had 1 hundred dollar bill left from my 4 band in tips from last night, but my bag and shoes was worth every penny. Then Nicholas drove me to my brownstone. I'm going to take a nap and then get ready for work, got to sleep with a warm rag between my legs Earl

Thursday, June, 29th

tore this pussy up but my body is at peace from his massage, but 1st I'm going to tell Emery I'm in, Miami here come Glammaris! Yes, I googled Emery's ass. He's words are real. I'm young and fill of cum but I ain't dumb! LOL! TTYL!

Friday, June, 30th

Last night was the some old bullshit. 10 minutes before I was going to walk out the door to go to work Naturel comes in my brownstone crying. I didn't want to but I asked her what was wrong. Still fighting with Black, over the same thing. They are so fried! He's threatening to financial cut her off. She needs for me to pet her up but I didn't have time for it. So I give it to her straight with no chaser. Either she was going to fuck Black and accept his female friends that he fucks and get some male friends of your own to fuck or only fuck Black while he do him and continue to cry, while he take care of you. I say fuck Black and get use to taking care of herself. Shit it's not that hard! Naturel is just like half of these chicks out here. I have never heard of a faithful side chick, have you? PYP!!! Naturel said I don't know love. She is right I don't know about loving someone more than I love myself! And I tell niccas don't love me, just fuck me, pay me or make me cum and keep your feet shuffling! And that's the bottom line to Naturel's problem, she is putting Black before herself. I left her with a lot of right to think about. Then I came out of my building to get in my ride from the car service guess who is in front of my building drunk begging for sex? No other than that damn Monty. I asked him did he have money for me? He took too long to answer so I jumped in the backseat of my ride. And fucking Nicholas is my driver for the night. Shit I had to fucking pay again. Some old bullshit. I could call another cab service but with this one I can request foreign cars and not be charged extra. Tonight I was feeling presidential, so Nicholas was driving an all-black Surburban with tinted windows. I popped a molly in the backseat. I was agitated. I had to calm down. Men like friendly, happy and horny dancers and the molly was going to make sure I deliver a bubble-ly dancer. I had to get myself to that light loose place. Nicholas running his fucking mouth as usual. Finally I got to club and I'm right on time. I was next to the main stage. The 1st song I danced to was *2 on by Tinashe.* I clear the stage of a bed of many 1 dollar bills and put them in my little satin drawstring bag. After my set I went to the locker room to change my outfit and drop the black satin bag off in my locker. I color coordinate my satin money bags, black, blue and purple are stage bags. The white ones are floor bags. This is how I know where I made what I made. I came out the locker room scoping the crowd for a private lap dance. Niccas be lined up. I make them wait while I change up right quick. Their dicks grow with anticipation I stop by the bar. Immediately a white guy named Kyle bought me a drink. He was shaky. He confessed this was his 1st time in a strip club. I love rookies. I convinced him a lap dance would calm his nerves. I took him to the red room after he paid the $50 that give us access to lap dance area in the club. Every private lap dance room had a theme. In the red room there in one chair sitting in the middle of the floor. I pushed Kyle scary white ass down in the chair. I circled around him like a true predator. I snatched his point Dexter glasses off his face and throw them on the floor. I started dancing in front of him. I put my right leg over his left shoulder. I grind my pussy in his face and grabbed the back of his head so he could smell my pussy. I took my leg down. I straddled across his lap. I grind my pussy on his hard dick as his face rested in between my tities. I cupped his face with my hands. I dropped my head back and moaned as if he was fucking me. I flipped around and straddled him from behind and grind my ass cheeks on his hard dick. I gently bounced my ass on his lap until my ass cheeks were clapping together. Kyle was breathing hard. I grind harder. Before you know it I could feel the warm spot on his khaki slacks, announcing he had cummed on himself. Kyle went in his back pocket, took out his wallet and handed my $100 dollar bill and 100 thank yous. Another satisfied customer. I went to locker room to baby wipe my ass off and changed outfits. I kept 10 different outfits in the locker. You never know what's going to happen in a night. I had an hour before hitting the main stage again. So I got another drink from the bar and went scouting for another Kyle type. I found 3 more Kyle types, another $100, $80 and $50 in tips. I change yet again for my 2nd set. I grind to Usher's classic "*Do it to me.*" I collected my paper and 5 more lap dances before I could even go downstairs and change. For my last set I took down the house with *Nicki's Anaconda.* I go all out like the purple rain of prince. Black always giving me that look like I went too far. For the finale I finger pop myself and let one groupie from around the stage lick my cream off my finger. Them niccas in there go stupid and throw mad money on the stage. Shit after I change and come back to the floor every nicca be lined up for a lap dance. every dance come along with a shots of liquor. Thursday night was a $2,100 night and I was extra lit. Yes I intentionally left out the hate from them bitches I work with to show I still made my money while they so busy watching me. I was feeling good so I popped another molly. Nicholas's mouth was moving but I couldn't hear nothing he was saying. I was floating. Sidney texted my phone. Let me give you the drop on Sidney. I meet him at my senior's party 3 years ago. He is a cousin to my former classmate Jessica. Jessica was no different than any other girl in high school. They all hated me. Little did they know I was rocking a little of my moms's clothes and a little of Naturel's shit but none the less I was still on fleek. And they hated on me. Any way you know Jessica told Sid I was all types of hoes. He was still interested but I guess to afraid of what might happen. So nothing ever happen but we still text each other from time to time. Tonight he wanted to meet up. It was 5 in the morning. Nobody meets up for conversation at this time of the morning. Its DTF time. That 2nd molly made me want to fuck real bad and Nicholas wasn't an option. So I had Nicholas pick Sid up and head back to my apartment. The ride to the apartment I was questioning Sid, trying to find out where his head was at. He was going on and on bout kids, wife and work. He needed me as a friend and not for a fuck. I was disappointed. As much as I try to hide my disappointment the more it showed. Nicholas dropped us off at my apartment. We get inside Naturel was all curled up on the couch like a wounded puppy but once she saw Sid, shorty popped up like a pop tart out of a toaster.. Now she is a ray of sunshine getting ready to prepare breakfast. Naturel is my homie but bitches like her make me sick. A men come in the room and they become some other bitch. Trying to impress and all type of other shit. I would've normally said something but Sid ain't interested in fucking anybody, he just wanted to talk. I hated to be a bitch about it but my flight to Miami leaves in 6 hours and I had shit to do. So I put Sid, non-fucking ass, out. And asked Naturel for her $700 for the rent. She telling some story about if she pay she'll be broke. Then I guess she'll be broke. FOH! Shorty is running around here with a 34 hundred dollar *Hermes* shoulder bag but can't pay her rent? She got use to Black paying her half of the rent that she didn't plan for a rainy day. So it sound very personal to me. I felt a little sorry for her I gave back $100 as a loan not as a good looks. I took a shower and then went to take care of Mr. Buster. Mr. Buster is a 71 year old man that lives in my moms's building. I pay his bills for him, pick up stuff from the store for him, and tidy up his apartment for him. I've been taking care of Mr. Buster for 3 years, after his wife died. He didn't have any living family. I had his social security check go direct deposit to his bank account, paid his bills right in front of him on his little tablet I got him last Christmas. He like playing the slot machines games. Sometimes he'll go outside and feed the birds or stop by the senior center around the corner to play bingo but that was as far as Mr. Buster traveled. The doctors and nurse come to see him, regularly, even his prescriptions were delivered to his door. I had wheels on meals pull up to his door with breakfast, lunch and dinner, to insure he was eating. Last month Mr. Buster had a true confession moment and told me that due to arthritis he could no later please himself. He said "I know dem young'ins pay a pretty penny to get you to fondle them but all I got is $200, plus the hundred I always pay you." Aww Mr. Buster was too cute, he was willing to spend his bingo winnings on me. It wasn't about the

Friday, June, 30th

money, I wanted to help him. Sucking his dick was like eating the last captain crunch floating around in the cereal bowl. But I sucked on that soggy dick with no shame and collect my coins on the way out. LML! The next stop was grease monkey Louie garage to collect my weekly pay of $300. I only had to take $400 out of my money to pay my bills. My half of the rent plus Naturel's half, Con Ed, the cable, and my cell phone bill were all paid. I still had an hour before I had to be at the airport. I called my car service to take me back to my apartment and then to 5th avenue. I needed a Gucci bathing suit for Miami right off the mannequin in the window, it was an irresistible floral two piece but you know me one is never enough. LOL! So I got another one in black with the signature red and green stripes, and I had to have the bathing suit like the black one in white, 3 Gucci bathing suits for $794.78, now that what I call a bargain. Of course they sent Nicholas ass again. I had to ask, was he the only driver? He was trying to prove himself to his father, blah, blah, blah. Shit where the fuck was Mohammad at? I use to hate jerking his curry smelling dick but I truly would jerk the shit out of that curry dick right now. I can't believe I gotta pay for another fucking ride. I was off to LaGuardia airport. I don't know if it was the molly or the fact that I never been out of New York that I couldn't keep still. I was like a kid in the candy store just amazed at the airport scenery. I had confess to Nicholas that I had no clue of where I was going or doing. He was kind enough to lead the way to the address on my boarding pass. It felt like I was walking for hours when it was only minutes. I started questioning Nicholas 's knowledge that he claim to have. It was all unfamiliar to me. Well I was familiar with being searched, just not at an airport. HA! I made it right on time. They were collecting tickets when I pulled up on the scene. Nicholas was lingering around after he handed me my Gucci tote. I walked off on Nicholas ass. I had already tip his ass. I didn't know why he was hanging around. What he was looking for? a hug? I said thank you when I didn't have to. As a driver your job is to carry fucking bags, am I wrong? The little gray tunnel you walk thru to get to the plane was scary shit. I felt like I needed a space suit. When I took the step onto the plane, there was a little gap and I could see how far we were actually off the ground. I was ready to turn my punk ass around but there were people behind

Friday, June, 30th

me. I didn't want other people to know I was chicken shit. I found my seat and clutched my Gucci tote. I packed extra lite it was a one night affair. I packed 4 stage outfit, they ain't much cloth, mostly string. 3 summer dresses, 3 pairs of shoes, toiletries and 11 hundred dollar bills. A flat iron, gotta keep this hair looking right. I got 3 more weeks with this hair before Gucci tighten up my wave again. I had a window seat. I was just staring out the window when this cute but short guy sits next to me. I clutched my bag tighter. "This a bloody 2 hour flight you gonna have to loosen up." Is what he said. I would go sistah on his ass with the head moving, talking out the side of my neck and finger pointing, you know the whole 9 yards but he had the cutest English accent. I said "excuse me" just to hear him talk. The plane took off and I didn't even notice. After he got us some drinks he talked nonstop. It was cute how he mange to get the word "bloody" into every sentence. He had just come from the museum in New York trying to pitch his deceased father's painting. He also paints. He would love to paint me, so he slurs. He lives in Miami with his mother and sister. He's 26, no kids and single. Besides his painting hobby he owns a real estate company. So why is he single? Something is wrong, I say he has a 4 by 4, 4 inches in length and 4 inches in girth dick aka a baby dick. I was intrigued by the accent but now I'm more curious bout that dick. The plane was cold and the goosebumps on my arms and legs told that I was freezing. Trenton wrapped his Blazer around my bare legs and offered to share his body heat with a bear hug. I accepted. I would've packed a blanket if I know it was going to be below zero on the plane. Here I am all cute up with a little juicy short romper and a pair of *Nike* dunks. His cologne on his neck danced in my weave. We joked, laughed, and talked while I laid in his arms. I could feel the vibration of his words from his chest bouncing off the back of my head. My fingers danced on the hairs on his forearm. And before I know it the plane had landed and I took Trenton's number. As soon as I came out the tunnel a woman was waving her arm in the air with her hand beckoning at me. I looked around to make sure her sign language was talking to me. I was so nervous but my pride won't let me show it. I was a long way from home. Trenton lingered around to insure my safety. He earned a texted by being a gentleman. I hug Trenton's sexy ass goodbye with promises that I would call or text when I was settle. The lady introduce herself as Tricky Nicky. She's Emery's assistant. "You're a cuter than Emery said! You might be the one! I'm gonna talk and you're going to listen. Save your questions to the end. We are on our way to the club. I want you to go straight to hair, make-up, and wardrobe. You are the 1st lady on Emery's left side. You got it?" I nodded. "Questions?" I shook my head from side to side to say no. She was a very beautiful curvaceous woman. She was wearing the hell out of of a white two piece short sleeve business suit. The killer was the red lip stick, red bottom and top pumps and a sick red clutch. She is sexy but her tone said she meant business. I'm not like other females who hate instead of complimenting. I shot a few at Tricky Nicky and she beamed with thank yous. I followed her into a H2 Hummer stretch limo. It was a silent ride. I looked out the limo's tinted window in amazement. The palm trees were 10 times more beautiful than on TV. When we got to the club, the five other woman looked me up and down. If looks could kill, my moms would be collecting donations for my funeral right now. The hate was strong and I hadn't said a word. Tricky Nicky lead me to hair, make-up and wardrobe. I was dressed in a similar white Dior gown as the other 5 ladies. "Places ladies, on the right, Snowflake, April, Sundae, on the left, Glammaris, Ruby, Kissy." In the center of us was Emery sitting on a throne holding a bottle of liquor. The ladies was positioned to lay out on white bear rug, bear head included, as I appear to be filling everyone glasses. The cameras keep flashing lights and there were bright lights on stands, the bright lights on all sides made it hot even with the AC on and Tricky Nicky dared us to sweat. At first I kept blinking at the flashing of the super bright light on the camera. It was way different then taking a selfie, I'll tell you that. I stop count after like 50 snaps. I felt like I was doing the robot in slow motion. "Hold your head to the right no a little to the left, hold it, hold it" FOH! I dance, fuck and suck. LOL. This shit was work. After 4 hours we were finally finished taking pics. Tricky Nicky dropped us off at a hotel near the beach. The "left" ladies was in one room and the "right" ladies were in another room. On each bed was a manila envelopes and a black plastic drawstring bag. I open the envelope 1st. I almost had a heart attack when I read the itinerary. Tonight,

Friday, June, 30th

Miami club, Saturday off the coast of Key West at a private event, Sunday in ATL, Monday in LA, and on Tuesday, 4th of July back in NY. 10 bands for 1 weekend of work. I immediately pulled out my phone to call Black, to make sure I'll still have a job on Monday when I return back home. He was acting stink. His main concern was his stupid medical form. I promise to take care of the damn form. I wasn't going to let Black ruin my good time out of town. So I just hung up the phone and started talking to my roommates for the weekend, Ruby and Kissy, try to find out what they were all about and what this job was all about. They weren't new to Emery's circuit. This was their 2nd yr., they were here last year same time. Basically we are Emery's trophies for the weekend. We wait on Emery and his guest in VIP. Our outfits were provided for us in the drawstring bags. I asked what Tricky Nicky meant by "the one". "Only 1 of the 6 ladies here will be selected to do the next 5 events as his one trophy. The trophy is mount high for the world to see. Stars are born from being Emery's trophy." They were giving me the drop, on who to talk too and who to just stay clear of. They told me last year they each walked away with 10 bands from the after parties in tips plus Emery 10 bands. I was curious of why Nicky has tricky in front of it. When they told me I know they were playing a joke on me. There's no way in hell that Tricky Nicky was a men. Her facial features were too soft, her ass too fat, but her breast told the tale of being fake. LOL! But nonetheless she was a woman by all standards in my eyes. Ruby is a pretty face red bone. 5'8 but no ass and no tities. They must've reiterated her beauty to point of no return cause she has the "look at me I pretty" attitude. I complimented her on her shoes and she relied "I know they are cutie." No thank you. She was a club hostess in Miami. She painted a perfect relationship with her daughter's father and a perfect life. Too bad her painted picture of hers is one I would never see. Pictures have a way of revealing the hidden truth. She went on and on about how great of a father her "Hubby" was to their daughter. Why do black woman do this, bigging up a man for taking care of his children, like he is doing something special. Don't get me wrong, you are suppose to appreciate a man that is into his children but praise, nah! Her IG page was like a sick obsession over him. "Chillin wit the hubby." "dinner wit the hubby. "Taking Princess to school wit the hubby." OMG!! We get it, you love your "Hubby." So annoying!!! Kissy was optimistic she believed that her side chick days to a 1 hit wonder rapper was almost over after 2 years because she was 2 weeks pregnant. Why do woman think trapping a nicca with a baby will make the nicca love them? Shit the quickest way to get rid of a nicca is to mention the word baby. Bitches force a baby on a nicca then call him a dead beat dad cause he don't interact with the kids but finical supports the kid. No bitch! You a dead beat bitch for putting your wants of a fantasy before the unborn kid. SMFH! Ms. Kissy is a model, who had posed for JC Penny and Macy's. She bragged about her playlist of rappers that she had played thru never realizing she was played and ejected. Both of them look down on strippers. Fuck them both I make my money the way I want to, off the grip of a dick or a pole. Stripping is a job like cashier or sales rep. Strippers work harder. We gotta have a face, hair, nails and super curves. And know how to word attract men or niccas attention. Then once you get the men's or nicca's attention you gotta finagle words so that it feels and sounds good. Shit it's a gift to be able to play around with words the way I do!

Friday, June, 30th

Strippers are on the come up, we on reality TV and trapping rappers. LMAO! Kissy and her hip hop recycled pussy had some nerve. Hating bitches are everywhere. Ruby and Kissy wanted to nap for the 3 hours, we had to our self before we had to be dressed and ready for the club tonight. And they should cause they were tried hoes. I wanted to go to beach but didn't want to go by myself so I texted Trenton. Trenton replied in less than a half a second. I let him know where I was at and where I wanted to go. He agreed on accompanying me to the beach. I went down to the lobby to meet him. When he walked up I almost passed out. His cuteness had raised by 5. On the plane I was blinded by his accent that I missed his curly sandy blonde hair with a hint of nicca and his light brown seashell eyes. Seashell eyes have a way of talking you into a daydream just like the sounds captured in seashells. We strolled down the beach where the water meet the land of sand. We were wandering thru his childhood. Story after story from the past, things that had happened on the sand that was under our feet. I found out that he picked up his accent at a co-ed private school in London. His father being an army man afforded him the opportunity. He floated into his current employment as a lucrative realtor. He offered to show me a beach house he was just displaying to potential buyers. It was property that he was selling for a client with a 30 percent commission. The beach house was made of glass and inside the furniture was all snow white. It was like looking at summer and winter at the same time. It was a fairytale house. Thru the two story glass walls the kitchen, dining and living room could be observed from outside. The stairs to the 2nd floor was visible but inside the room weren't. Trenton gave me a full tour of this incredible beach house. This house is the one we've all seen on TV and dreamed of living in. He had some wine left from when he was captivating the potential buyers earlier. He poured each of us a glass. And then offered me bread and cheese. The cheese smelled like shit and looked crazy. It had blue specks. I refuse to try it but he pressed on, "How will you enjoy your bloody life if you don't try new things? To have life in not living. The bloody experience is living life!" so I tried the stink cheese. I must admit it wasn't as bad as it looked. Bitter like extra sharp cheddar but left a salty smelly taste in my mouth. He insisted I sipped the wine. The mixture of the "Gorgonzola" European cheese and the sweet port wine on my taste buds came together nicely like peanut butter and jelly. I laid out on the white mink floor rug. I was mesmerized by the glass walls. I stare at the different people walking by, the sea waves crashing on to the beach sand looked like soda fizz, the sky glowed cotton candy light blue and the clouds fluffy like marshmallows. The sun's feet prints were bubble gum and orange slices colored, the slash of sun's foot prints of candy colors appeared randomly. The sight of beauty was sweet eye candy. The silky fur was pleasing my skin, I was rubbing my bare legs against the mink rug. I was wearing my white Gucci bathing suit with a light oversized knitted sweater and Tory Burch flip flops on my feet. I asked how much did the house cost? Just out of curiosity. A whole lot of millions. Trenton also like the house. He said the house has been on the market for 6 months cause he couldn't bring himself to sell it. Mind you, he claim to have only come to the house with buyers. After showing them the house he falls in love with the house every time. This was my only time to the house and I had fell in love with it too. Laying on the white mink rug looking out at the scenery it gave to feeling of wanting to cuddle up and smooch all day as if I was in high school puppy love. Being surrounded by all the white made it heavenly. I asked him, why don't he just buy the damn house? With the 30% discount. Shit if I had the funds I would definitely buy this house, not only because the house was ode amazing but because of the feeling it gives me. He said "This bloody house is a fine body of art and should be admired and adored and left alone. No one should own art just praise it and cherish its existence." Maybe it was his accent but his words touched me like a feather across my nipples. His passion in his words combine with his accent was more than flirtatious. The smile in his light brown seashell eyes were talking dirty to me. He admits to being a sex exhibitionist and would love to have sex in this house in the living room right in front of the windows. His verbal enjoyment of having sex in public intensify the glow of his caramel skin. I confessed I would be too focus on the people watch to actually have sex and enjoy it. Could you have sex in the open with people watching? He said the right lover would stimulate me to the point that I wouldn't care who was watching. I laugh in his face really tried not to but just couldn't hold it. He took my laugher as a challenge. "Will 3 thousand bloody pound make you give it a bloody try?" The words came straight out his mouth with his accent on strong but the competitive nature spoke thru his seashell eyes. He meant to have said for 3 bands. I was being indecisive. I know I'm a stripper and I don't have a problem with taking my clothes off and I shouldn't have a problem with fucking in public but I do have a problem fucking on the beach, literary! The sun was still out, kids running around. I still was very hesitate, until he laid out the 30 crispy hundred dollar bills out in front of me to prove he wasn't all talk. He initiated by folding his right hand's fingers with my left hand's fingers. He then knead down over me folding his left hand's fingers with my right hand's fingers. His supple lips kissed my forehead while showering me with compliment. "You are a body of fine art. Your skin is that of an Egyptian goddess. Your eyes sparkle like princess cut diamonds. Your highness, may I be of service to you?" I nodded quickly responding to the whispers of his seashell eyes but my mind was still not sure. "Close your eyes and open you senses." I still was very shaky even after seeing the money but his poetic words under the accent influence put me at ease. I had word intoxication. He used his supple lips to kiss each eyelid close. He kissed my nose. His lips graced my lips before he kissed my chin. I could sense his presences but I felt the affection in the descriptive words he used to praise my facial features. His tender breath caressed my skin. His supple lips planted a kiss where my neck and shoulder met. The warmth of his lips gave me chills. It felt like the airs of our spirits were connecting. I had peeked and peeped he peeled me out of my clothes. I fidgeted a little at the thought of strangers taking a peek. "You are a picturesque, that I would never change a thing, you are bloody beautiful the way you are." His gentle words calmed my jumping nerves. As he poetically label the fine parts of art on my body he planted his supple lips in the center of my breast. His intoxicating words gave me another drink as his breath danced across my nipples. My nipples stood up and begged for his attention. He taunted my nipples by coating them with praises instead of touch. His sensual breathing danced down to my navel teasing my skin. He filled my navel with his warm tongue. The wetness of his tongue cause me to leak between my legs. I squeezed his hands as I came. The sensation of awaited contact exploded. He unfolded our hands and held both of my hands above my head with his left hand. His soft fingertips fiddled and twiddled with the liquefied anticipation between my legs. The intercourse of his words in my ear caused my skin to beg for satisfaction. His breath toyed with my sexually charge nipples. I verbally begged for his dick. His fingers manipulated my privates to cry uncontrollable for his dick. He tormented my skin with sexual airs. He spanked my creamy pussy with his hard dick. The slapping sound made my pussy pant and my mouth plead loudly for the dick. Finally he filled me with latex coated hard pleasure, I was craving. He continued his game by giving me some and quickly it's taken away. He provoked the inner sexual beast in me. He finally let my hands go and I grabbed him by the ass cheek to prevent him from moving. I held him tight keeping the dick inside while I grind my panting pussy on it. A gush of cream came on to his dick. He guided my hand to fondle "the gooch" maybe it was his accent or maybe I was confused by my racing hormones. He directed my hand to caress the skin between his balls and asshole. The more I massage the "gooch" the harder the strokes. In the middle of my creamy explosion he had steered my finger into his asshole. My finger being in his asshole cause him to cum. The moment was broke. I was full aware of the few specters in the audience. I collected my clothes and my money as Trenton lays out on the mink rub with full satisfaction. I speed walked across the sand back to hotel. I could feel people point and whispering I didn't dare pick my head up to look at nobody. Okay he had an average size dick. An average hard dick is 7 inches in length and about 5 inches in girth. I give Trenton about 7 and a quarter, but he had me so thirsty it feel like a 10 foot pole. I enjoyed Trenton's mental fuck but he wasn't getting his calls answered. And now I know why other chicks ain't beating down his door. That man got some sugar in him. The only gooch I know was the bully from the show *Different Strokes*. Don't ask, one day I couldn't find the remote and got all caught up watching the stupid show then I couldn't turn if I wanted to. When I got to the hotel room, Ruby and Kissy were still sleep. There was still an hour to kill. I quietly showered. I think I watched my finger 20 times. I don't know if it was a mental thing but my finger still smell like shit to me. Even the 30 hundred dollar bills smell like shit, giving a new meaning to dirty money. LOL! I throw on a sundress and went to the hotel bar. I had a shot of henny. I need to wash down my sex-perience with Trenton. Malcom, the bartender keep me company. His nickname was X. X is a native of Miami. He deejays on Saturdays. He's a real hip-hop head. With all the tattoos covering X's skin I was sure he was a punk rocker, see never judge a book by its cover. We played guess that lyric. X had did his homework he knew lyrics from Common to Kendrick. Shit he got me stuck a few times, not bad for a white boy. X was a breath of fresh air after a shitty situation, literally. I said good bye to X. I went back to my room and curled my hair. Ruby and Kissy were running around like pigeons. The outfit is provided to us all we had to add was hair, make-up and shoes. The outfit is black boy shorts with Emery's logo on the right ass cheek and a belly shirt with the Emery's logo on the front. I added spice to the little outfit by rocking black fishnet stockings and my fresh out the box muilt-colored glitter Christian Louboutin heels. You know the ones, I just copped the other day. Ruby and Kissy hating

"You can't wear that, it's against the rules. Maybe you should of read the packet instead of chilling. Tricky Nicky don't allow us to change the uniform." Bitch I left my moms back in New York and I read the packet waiting on Trenton nasty ass in the lobby. In the packet it say you can't alter the uniform. It say no jewelry. Nowhere do it say no stockings. I don't feel like I changed the uniform. I didn't want be no sextuplets with this hating ass bitches. I added my own spices. I don't see a problem, do you? Tricky Nicky knocked on the door and entered with the "right" females, the three of them were snickering at me. Ruby responses to their snickers by saying "I told her." Tricky Nicky just started talking "Tonight you ladies are representing Emery brand, that comes with a lot responsibilities. Put your cell phones on vibrate. You're going to see a lot of celebrities. You must act like you see celebrities every day. You are not allowed to take selfies or ask for autographs. No small talking with any of the guest. You are only allowed to talk to myself or Emery. But you can expect tips at the after party if selected. Your job is to serve liquor in the VIP area and only the VIP area. Do y'all got it?" We all nodded together. She starts to walk out but turns to me to say "Cute Glammaris, I like a woman who embrace her own style." Them tired hoes were sick in the face. I followed Tricky Nicky out the room with my head in the air. We took the same H2 limo from earlier back to the club. The inside and under the outside of the limo had a neon green glow. #fleek! Emery was awaiting us in the back seat. Emery asked would I like to sit next to him. Them sick hoes faces looked like throw up. LMAO! Emery like the fishnets too. When we pulled up to the club it was a mob outside. Tricky Nicky wasn't getting out the H2. She told us she'll pick us up later. We got out the limo in order. Emery first, right side hoes, then myself and the left side hoes. Camera's flashing lights all in our face. Shit it made me feel like I was a real celebrity. Not the hood celebrity status when random men and niccas running down on me for a pics. Ode annoying. We paraded down the red carpet on the side walk. The red carpet was protected by a velvet rope down the right and left side of the red carpet. Inside the club look completely different at night then during the day. In the day light it looked like the club, Emerald, was under reconstruction with open wiring hanging from the ceiling but at night the wiring turned into green lighting. The lighting of the club made it look stars where falling from the sky inside the club. It was so charming. Tricky Nicky didn't prepare us for the A list celebrities that came thru VIP to congratulate Emery on his new Liquor addition. From the likes of Mr. Elba himself to Denzel Curry going hard. This nicca from MIA was up in NY for a summer and I was fucking with him, his favorite song was "Threatz" by Denzel Curry. I was hype to see him but some of the other girl didn't know who he was. It was an amazing diverse crowd. Music breeds unity. It was my pleasure to pass out bottles to this elite superstars. The experience made me want to be a part of the guest list and not a high class waitress at the event. With this type of crowd there is always an after party. Emery selected the "right" side bitches to join him while Tricky Nicky took the "left" side back to the hotel. Ruby and Kissy were sick it was only 1 am and their night was over. As for me my night had just begun. I caught up with X. He was deejaying at a spot and invited me. This club was a down grade from Emery's club. It was a hood party, with hood bitches and hood niccas. After Trenton I needed to be fucked by

Friday, June, 30th

a hood nicca. I got a drink at the bar as I scouted the crowd. Crossing my finger I find exactly what I was looking for. I left the club with nothing. SMFH! I didn't see anyone with the proper credentials to get this pussy. I got back to room at around 3 am and the "right' bitches were being dropped off by Tricky Nicky. Tricky Nicky just came in the room to say goodnight. "Tomorrow we set sail at 2 pm. Get your beauty rest, what are writing?" I told her my thoughts. "You shouldn't be thinking you should be sleeping and if you not sleeping you're working! If I see that book again I'm gonna burn it! Got it?" I believe she'll really will do it, so I'm gonna holla when I get back to NYC! I PROMISE TO GIVE YA THE DROP ON EVERYTHING! TTYL!

Tuesday, July 4th

I'm back! Did you miss me? MAAAAAAAAAAAAAAAAAAAAAAD STUFF HAPPENED!!! Happy Independence Day! You know I'm going to put you on! Saturday I was still in Miami, remember? At like around noon, Tricky Nicky came to our rooms with a change of outfit because one of the guest didn't approve of our uniforms and offered their designer brand. The new form fitting metallic emerald green dress stopped at the thighs. The front of the dress came up to the collar bone and the back had a V opening down to the crack of my ass. The dress was runway couture. I felt model-ish in the fabric. Some of these bitches was sick. They couldn't wear their push up bra to hold them soggy tities. LMAO! Are they nipple was crossed eyed? LOL! I just had naturally perky tities with large dark areolas. Of course you know I had to put my stink on it with my gold-issh glitter Christian Louboutin and my Vikki's gold body shimmer. I was glad I packed them. I had 3 pair of shoes and toiletries galore. These jealous hoes kept screaming "This is there 2nd and 3rd yr. on this tour with Emery", so why you hoes only pack 2 pair of shoes and like 1 outfit? Them hoes be looking me over, I dare one of them to try me.

I'm a lover not a fighter but the hate is so strong it makes me feel like a killer. I wonder who the drama queen was that made us change our uniform to their designer dresses? I was so valid with my spiral curls on fleek. No gas my eye brows came out perfect. #fleektothemax! LOL! We walked in a group to meet up with Tricky Nicky at the beach loading dock. Now these hoes want to open up about the after party the night before. Sundae was bragging how she had dick suckered her way in to a rapper's video, filming next week. 1st let me say I'm not a hater! I'll suck a dick or flip a clit for what I want too but I'm so low key. I do what I do, and if you know what I do, you watching me cause I ain't talking bout it, I'm doing it. And 2nd I gets mine up front! Video filming next week? FOH! Next week will come and she'll be fighting thought security just to get in the gate while that nicca acting like he never met her. Not for me! I would of use some of my poise to massage some words so he could feel it. Sommin like "Keep that dick dry til the video so I can make it rain on you." I've used that same line at the club to curve ballers that have already made it rain on me, and wanted to fuck. FOH! If it works, then work it, right? April is another right side hoe. April was straight up delusional. She let some cute face talk her into some fairytale mind set, where unicorns and mermaids live. The same old basic faithful side bitch drama. "He's gonna leave his wife, someday." But someday ain't 1 of the days in a week! LOL! Clown bitches for real. If it's too good to be true then a charismatic tongue lied to you. I do give April more respect than Kissy. April has gotten a crib and a car out of her married boo ass. April couldn't wait to get to Atlanta, her hometown, to show of her pussy winnings. Snowflake was talking Ruby and Kissy heads off about her hometown LA. I had only been a day away from home for 1 day and for woman like us whom get up and go as we please it felt like a week. We met up with Tricky Nicky at the dock. She like my body glitter so much that she asked me to share with the plain hoes. We all loaded on to Emery's "yacht". Ruby had called it a boat and Ms. Snowflake informed her it was a "yacht." LOL! The "yacht" is two stories high. The second floor has a dining area. On the first level there's a dance floor under the dining area. The back deck on the 1st level has emerald colored love seats and cushioned beach chairs. Everyone were on the deck enjoy the semi-fast sail to the coast of Key West. The 6 of us was going to serve Emery's liquor to about 30 guest. Tricky Nicky handed us some pretty rhinestone cover tong sandals for us to wear. I was mad that I had to take off my *Christian Louboutin* for some payless sandals. The club celebrities from last night was nothing compare to exclusive elite super stars that was seated here that evening. Even though I wasn't sitting at the table with Danzel, B or Hov, I was rubbing elbows with them. I wanted to be a part of this crowd. In between serving I was being a creep and listening to their conversations. I tell you no lies they are regular people with money. Some of them didn't look like they looked on TV. Some of them were down right hideous. 100% filtered images on the TV screen. After lunch the celebrities scattered around the yacht. It was like we were playing hiding go seek to ask them if they want anything. Before you know it night had fell and the light on the bottom of the yacht lit up, like H2 limo. The green glow on the water was spectacular. It was pretty romantic. Some celebrities took swims. Which meant I had to grabs towels. The dance floor inside the yacht turned up, and all the tropical fish swimming under the yacht could be seen through the transparent dance floor. After everyone was over the beauty in the dance floor and liquor was flowing heavy through their systems, they begin to dance to the music. This was the best part of the experience for me to see unordinary people be ordinary and were enjoying themselves. It was a stunning sight. The yacht docked around 10 ish. We were swept to the hotel and straight to the Miami airport. It happened so fast, I felt like I had whip lash. You know I get nervous with that damn tunnel to the plane but I walked through like a pro in front of them jealous hoes. Snowflake is a right side hoe. She sat next to me on the flight to Atlanta from Miami. 2 hours and 15 minutes of her mouth running about LA. When we landed in Atlanta Tricky Nicky was awaiting us. She gave each of us an envelope of petty cash, and said she see us at 8pm at the club. "Please don't forget our receipts." We had $200 each to hold us down for the day and what we didn't send had to be given back. It was 8 am we had the whole day to ourselves. Of course the first stop in the H2 was the Westin hotel. Ours rooms were on the 70th floor. The view was miraculous. We could see the whole city and beyond. Our hotel room view was like standing on the top floor of New York's empire state build. April invited all of us to her home. The other jealous hoes declined. Pure haters! Can't stand to see anybody winning! I was excited to see her pussy's winnings, so I went. April called her sponsor slash man to pick us up. I sat in the back seat quiet as a church mouse as they went back and forth about him no answering her text. Side hoe drama! PYP! As a side hoe your position is to stand on the sideline until you are called into the game! PYP! He dropped us both off at April's house with promises to return. I didn't believe him and I hoped April didn't believe him either. April's house from the outside didn't look no different than a house back home in Queens but inside was another story. She had marble floors, high tech appliances, rooms for a closet space and a pretty pool. Her son's room was like a studio apartment. He had every latest gadget and toy. Her 4 year old son was at her mother's house. April's house was incredible. April was happy to be in her city, I could tell cause she couldn't stop smiling even after getting into with her "man". She made 2 glasses of mimosa, one for me and one for herself. She turned on the radio. We sipped and sang alone to the songs playing until we were bored. We decided to spend our little $200. So April took me to an underground mall in her fire red *Lexis* coup. The underground had everything there. I shopped around, picked up some nick nacks. What really caught my eye was statue of man sitting reaching for the statue duck. The struggle was in the statues facial expression and you could tell he didn't have much by his clothes but was willing to lead a hand to the duck. The gesture was inspiring. I was feeling warm inside. We then went to pick up April's son from her mother's house. We made it right on time for the noon fountain ring show in the "downtown" area of ATL. It was beautiful. I was more thrilled then the 4 year old little boy. We then went to the aquarium. We walked through tunnels that had the water and the fish swimming around you besides the smell it was some romantic shit. My pussy was swimming from the ambiance. April dropped me back off at the hotel. Ruby and Kissy was getting ready to grab something to eat with the "right" side bitches. I declined to go even though they didn't offer. LMAO! They was tight! I took a nice bubble bath. I try to soak the horniness out my soul but really needed to be fuck by a hood nicca with a bad attitude. I took a nap trying to sleep the thirstiness off. But woke up famished. I had to put my pussy to the side and got to work. Emery's Atlanta club looks just like the club in Miami. Same setting and everything. And of course all the elites came out. From Usher to Joseline. Shit, I wish I could snap just one selfie with Joseline turning her tantrum up! LOL! I love her! She straight don't give a fuck and will throw them hands, whether she win or lose! #SALUTE! And you know with Emery there's always an after party and unfortunately I wasn't selected again. ☹ Emery picked April and Sundae to accompany him to the after party. I was glad I wasn't selected. I had to feed my desirous pussy. My pussy was on a late night thirsty bully mode. I entered the bar with a black thigh squeezing dress. I sat on the far right side of the bar. I ordered a drink. I sat and sipped. I was just waiting for the right one. My last sex-perience with Trenton wasn't one I care to remember but couldn't seem to forget. I need to be fucked not taunted with. Don't judge me! I'm not a hoe I just fuck a lot. LMAO! Ginuwine said "As long as you protect yourself and do it right." After 2 hours and 4 drinks I had finally lined up a target. Black suede construction boots on his feet, fitting but not tight Levi jeans slightly sagging off his ass, smile on the rocks, and an original Yankee fitted on his head. I was curious why a man in ATL would be rocking a Yankee fitted. But to be truthful it was his structure of muscles busting out his v-neck black t-shirt that caught my pussy's attention. He was sitting at the end of the bar for 45 minutes nursing a glass of a dirty spirit to soothe some emotional pain. I sent him a bottle of black Belaire. The wine will soften the pain and harden his dick. The waiter took the bottle of wine over to Mr. Yankee fitted and pointed to me. Mr. Yankee fitted then got up and walked over to me. I had to finesse the situation so it appeared like he picked me up, when in reality I lined him and he didn't even know it. The southern tang in words rolled of the tip of his tongue. He insisted that I share the bottle of wine with him. I granted his wish. We laughed and talked for like a 1 hour and a half, the bottle was done. He insisted that he pay for the bottle, since he practically drunk it by himself. He gave me a hundred dollar bill when the bottle only cost me $50. It looked like I would have to just come out and ask for the dick, cause he hadn't took the bait. SMH! I thought maybe he would've bitten by now but his southern hospitality wouldn't let him be a New York hound and take this pussy offering in his face. I said I needed fresh air to get him outside the bar. Under the moon light his southern chocolate skin had a scar across his left cheek, I've been on his right side the whole time. The scar made my pussy chirp at the southern bell. I played more drunk then I really was just to brush up against his southern stiff rod. He walked me to back to the hotel, like a true gentleman. He walked on left side near the curb, southern tradition a man's hospitality is to keep the woman on the inside out of harm's way. The gentleness combine with his southern roughness had my pussy singing. We passed his candy paint truck sitting on 24's. I told him I would love to invite him up for a night cap but I was sharing the room with my friends. He wasn't satisfied with leaving me in the lobby and neither was I. I wanted to fuck! I went to get on the elevator and he followed. I thought his southern smoothness was forcing him to walk me to my room door. I was looking at myself in the elevator's mirror walls. I looked like I had been drinking but wasn't drunk. My hair wasn't a mess, even though it should be, I had dropped my head on this man shoulder numerous times along with playful taps to his physique all night. I was impressed with my image staring back at me, my make-up was as fresh as when I put it on. #fleek! When the elevator doors closed it was like a bell to start the match had rung. His left hand grabbed a hand full of my weave from behind and backed me into his rod. The stiffness of the rod pressed up against my ass excited me in more ways than one. My head fell back onto the pillow of muscles on the left side of his chest. He savagely kissed and licked the right side of my neck. I gently placed my hand on the top of his Yankee fitted silently cheering him on. His tongue danced inside out my ear, I moan to the breathing music of lust in the air. His unrestrained craving made my pussy moist. His right hand viciously handled both of my breast. The intensity of his sexual energy caused me to sprinkle cream onto my g-string. To heighten his sexual energy I sucked on his index finger on his right hand. His grip on my weave got tighter. His sexual energy prompted him to extend his left hand without letting his grip on my weave go and leaned me forward with a swift movement. He used his right foot to kick my legs apart and pulled my g-string to the right side with his right hand. He is a crafty man. He unbutton his jeans and slipped into a condom all with his right hand, I watched him through the mirror. He entered my pussy with an untamed stab by the southern stiff rod. He rammed the whole thing deep inside my pussy. His left hand gripped my weave and his right hand took hold of my right hip. It wasn't enough that I was taking the reckless beating from the rod. He slapped my left ass cheek and shouted "Fuck me, shawty!" the southern tang in his voice jumped pass his bottom row of gold covered teeth. I tossed my pussy on his rod with force. The more I pitch this pussy the harder he hit. He used his right hand to lift my right leg. His left hand's grip on my weave pressed my face up against the mirror and battered my pussy with ruthlessness constant blows. My pleasure was voiced by my heavy patting. The condensation build up on the mirror glass like the explosion building up in the solid rod. He was driving the rod so deep up in my pussy it was hitting my voice box. I couldn't speak. It was sexual sensuality being painfully good. I was enjoying the moment to the max. The sexual aggression made my pussy pour creamy delight all over his rod and dripped down his balls. The squishy sound of rod digging deep into my soaking wet pussy oozing with cream cause me to climax. He pulled the rod out of my wet pussy. He pulled the condom off, all with his right hand. His left hand still was filled with my weave. He turned me around and bought me to my knees all with his grip. I inhaled the rod charged with the sexual energy. His grip controlled the speed of my mouth gliding up and down his shaft. His hips gyrated to warmth of my mouth. His right hand joined his left hand and grasp a chunk of my weave. With the rod deep in my throat it injected its southern cream and his mouth let out a series of loud moans. I pulled down my dress as he pulled himself together. He used the inside of his t-shirt to clean the southern cream residue off the side of my mouth, like a southern gentleman. He picked the condom up off the floor, wrapped it in tissue and hid it in pocket. He then hit the emergency stop button, I was so caught up I didn't even realize the elevator wasn't moving. The door to the elevator opened on my floor. There were 3 elderly guest and a bellhop. "Ay man, it just stop and start by itself." Is what Mr. Yankee fitted offered as an excuse for the hold up. I just snickered under my breath. one of the elderly guest shouted "They were in there fucking!" I wonder what gave us up the scent of sex that fogged the elevator, my make-up smeared on the elevator's mirror wall, or the drops of cream on the elevator floor? I caught a glance of myself in the mirror. My hair was a mess flying all over my head, my make-up looked like clown make-up, my eyeliner was running and my lipstick all out of the lip line. I looked like I just got the shit fucked out me. You ain't never been fucked if you ain't been fucked by a southern man. LMAO! I hugged him good night and thanked him for the fuck. It was what I needed when I needed it. He fucked me like he missed me but never met me before tonight. Damn, I wish I know Mr. Yankee fitted name, I would definitely love to fuck him again. Maybe I'll give him a call the next time I'm in ATL, he had given me his number on a hundred dollar bill. I've would of fucked him for free the $100 was a bonus. Thanks tho! LOL! I slept like a baby that night. Mr. Yankee fitted was good shit! I woke up all chirpy like the southern birds singing in the air. You know them bitches didn't like that. I was in great spirits. I was packed and ready to leave to the airport by the time Ruby and Kissy woke up. I hope LA had some good dick to offer. The flight from ATL to LA was 5 hours 8 minutes long. I thought New York was fast pace LA is 10 times worst. See in NY it's on the side walk where disrespect was at its highest level in LA the disrespect was in the street, cars switching lanes at 90 miles per hour or sitting in traffic for eternity. At least in NY a person would stop to give you directions, these mofos wouldn't even give me eye contact. LA is the city of broken dreams, when NY is the city where dreams are made. You know Snowflake would die if she didn't give us a tour of her state of mind. Don't you hate when somebody say "I'll give you a tour of the city" but all they show you is their favorite attractions. Well Snowflake was different. We went to walk down Hollywood boulevard with the red stars of fame under our feet, star glazing at unforgettable talent. Snowflake head our feet to the Chinese Theater. I was amazed and took plenty selfies. It looked like an authentic dojo. With its dragon statues and golden doors, it was just like in the movie. Of course we were star stricken by the foot and hand prints of legends embedded in the side walk. Out of the ones we read the one that stood out to me was Will Smith's "Change the world" I didn't know what it meant but I know it meant something. Either I'll figure it out or it will figure me out. Our next stop was Universal studios. We all piled up in an XL golf cart. We drove thru movie sets. It was far different from seeing things thru the TV. The best to me was the bates hotel set. It reminded me of my moms. This is her favorite movie she would've loved this. And I want to know who goes to LA without seeing the infamous "HOLLYWOOD" letters? These bitches was really trying to dead me on my fucking adventure. We had exactly 2 hours before having to be at the hotel. Fuck LA traffic!!! I straight got on my bully and told the H2 drive where I wanted to go. We made it back only 10 minutes' late, and what. This was the 4th party with Emery. I got excited by the celebrities but now I recognized them as regular people with regular life and regular problems they just have an irregular talent that they are blessed to share with the world. I guess I've learned to just appreciate their irregular talent. People are too nosy! Love celebrities for their irregular talent, not their personal life. When I go shopping I got a favorite sales rep I like the way she do her job, I don't care who she smashing or who's her baby daddy? Celebrities should get the same respect but it ain't like that. SMH! After we served Emery liquor all night, at about 2 in the morning the after party was set to begin at a secret location. Yup I was skipped over yet again. I wouldn't let that ruin my night. I zoed Ruby and Kissy into going to a lounge. 1st off every nicca had their eyebrows arched, eyeliner and blinding white teeth. They inspiring actors pretend to know themselves. The females with laced weaves and tight attitudes. Female models that can't picture their own thought. Everybody acting extra cause they were an extra in some movie or show. I had no other option but to rock my pussy to sleep with the thoughts of Mr. Yankee fitted. LOL. The 4 days of partying and traveling caught up with me. I slept the whole 5 hour flight. The time zone thing really fucked me up. We got on the plane in LA at 6 am but when we got off in NY it was 2:30 pm but the flight is only 5 hours. Yeah it fucked you up too, right? Tricky Nicky was at JFK airport when we disembark from the plane. Tricky Nicky was waving her hand like we couldn't see her. Even in NY a 6 foot sassy chick standing on 9 inch heels was very hard to miss. By us walking up to her it was like someone's foot hit the play button on her mouth. "I'm going to talk and walk, keep up. Y'all only have 3 hours before the party starts. It a rooftop day party. Not saying I don't trust you gurls to handle beating your face and to lay her hair, but I got a glam squad waiting on yous at my apartment directly across from the lounge. I have some runarounds so treat my home with care." There was no shade between the right and left ladies. Together we shined bright. We were excited it was our last day of work. We will return to our lives 10 stacks richer. I will never say it out loud but I was going to miss them all for different reason. The only Snowflake in LA naïve personality and tone. Her voice reminded me of a 5 year old kid. I gave Ms. Sundae my number and IG and begged her to keep me posted on the video shoot thingy, ROFLMAO! And Ruby's snotty ass with her picture perfect POTD selfies every morning. Kissy sick pregnant ass, every move, every smell, just everything bothers her. IMO shawty needs an AB ASAP! April I was going to miss most of all we bonded a little something. She's played the game and didn't let the game play her. A lot of females and males play the game and then want to change the rules when they see fit. NOOOO! That's not how you play the game. If you start the game in one position than that's the position you play the entire game. That the rules. Side hoes looking to be a main chick or Main chicks being side hoes WTF? Don't ever do a different positions unless it is in the bed. LMAO! Would you ask Trigger to host a hoedown or ask Tunechi to drop an opera LP? NO! Tricky Nicky has a cutie XL one bedroom apartment on west 57th street. As promised the glam squad was on deck. And beat your gurl face in! Laid this tired weave down. 13 days and counting to new hair! We were being the nicest we ever been to each other. We ran across the street to Above 6 at 6 and was right on time. The rooftop interior design gave off a comfy feel, with the throw pillows and candles. My lips wanted to snuggle with a cutie I spotted out my peripheral. He stood about 5"8 in height something like 50 cent wide. Eyebrows like plush velvet over sliced almond shaped eyes, long seductive eye lashes, a quarter size brown mole on his left cheek looked like a chocolate chip. The complexion of a perfectly baked cookie, not too dark and not too light. Mr.

Tuesday, July 4th

Chocolate chip was bodying an all white linen suit. Looking just heavenly! Every time the wind blow the imprint in the front of his pants make my pussy whistle. I wish I wasn't working so my pussy could rundown on him, properly. LOL! My pussy has a sweet tooth and he had a long thick sweet treat. I guess he could feel my eyes undressing him, cause he turned and winked at me. My pussy winked back with a leaky eye. I took a gamble and slipped him my number. I gambled getting caught by Tricky Nicky and him not calling but that was one cookie I want to take a bite out of! I was breed and born in NYC and I never saw the fireworks on the 4th of July. So I was kinda excited for 8 pm. The explosion of lights in the dark sky. For some strange reason while my eyes stare in amazement at the beautiful colors burst and pop Will Smith's words flashed in my vision "Change the world". The firework that starts with one ball and spray out in to hundreds of lines of light on both sides. It definitely was a message in there but it didn't hit me but I'll catch it later. Now that I have witness the fireworks I'll never miss it again. While the fireworks were blasting in the sky. There were sparkles lit in Mr. Chocolate chips eyes. He was pinwheeling my frame. He licked his lips in approval of his view and my pussy felt the lick from his tongue. The party ended at 10pm but the spot wasn't completely empty until 11. Tricky Nicky delivered as promised 10 bands. 100 crispy hundred dollar bills. "The one" we be notified by mail. We said our goodbye's after hugging each other. My pussy was on that late nite thirsty bully shit. My pussy couldn't forget the image of Mr. Chocolate chip. So, I went to check Earl as promised. Earl is the type to hold me to a promise. But to be truthful I need and wanted to be fucked. And it had to be a nicca that could compete with Mr. Yankee fitted. Of course my luck I ran into Jah, ANNOYING! black ass in front of the building. Jah be trying to be polite but I had one question, why is he even talking to me? He flapping his lip about Monty's lame ass coming to the club looking for me. Monty would tell his story to anybody that would listen, I'm just mad Jah was listening. "Wow, you charged ole boy a stack? I know you not gonna do me like that, right?" Well Jah was wrong I'll charge his ass 15 hundred. To be honest Jah didn't have the proper credentials to get this pussy and he damn sure didn't have 15 hundred. So I ended the conversation with

Jah cause it wasn't about dollars so it didn't make sense. When I got to Earl's crib it was a few nicca having a smoke fest, the cloud was loud. I know it was a dub for me to getting some dick from Earl's ugly ass. I could've made Earl put these niccas out but I'm extra quiet about fucking Earl's ugly ass. I still chilled there silently and joined in on the loud fog. Earl, Alfonzo aka Alf, James aka Funny were live entertainment. 3 broke, busted and disgusting niccas arguing over a fucking video game. Alf really look like the 80's show muppet, Funny look like nickelodeon's Doug Funny cartoon and yall ready know what Earl ugly ass look like. Alf was the type of nicca that post pics bout load this and loud that on his IG page but coughing up a lung on every pull of the blunt. Besides Funny looking funny he was funny. All day long he cutting on somebody when he is the funniest looking nicca I've ever seen. Somebody knocked on the door and guess who it was? Mr. Christopher Peterson. Christopher Peterson is the last person I expected to see at ugly Earl's apartment but that 2k basketball, Maddan football video game and loud cause people who would never speak come together. I have always wanted some Christopher Peterson along with every other woman he come in contact with. Mumm Christopher Peterson, I like to have him for dinner, desert and breakfast. Christopher Peterson was every niccas nightmare and every woman's dream. A star athlete, 6'5 coated in creamy butterscotch complexion, and the gift of Gabe that will make you gag. LOL! When I was beginning my freshmen year in high school it was Christopher Peterson's senior year. By the time I was comfortable in my own skin he was graduating from the school. I just missed him by 1 year. But we've seen each other once or twice from a distance and he was definitely interested. Seeing him face to face had my pussy high school blushing. Christopher Peterson went on to play college basketball from high school. I watched a few games on TV but my pussy couldn't handle it. He played 1 year in the NBA D-League after college and for the past two years he plays on a professional overseas team. Christopher Peterson pull up in the hood from time to time. Christopher Peterson step to me, up front with his game face on. "I wanna see all the shit I done heard." Is what he said. I came back with "Well, what you heard?" "You are superb with your sweet lips." "Tru, I'm nice with both sets but I make my bands of the grip of these lips, so whatcha working with?" See I would've fuck Christopher Peterson for free just cause I wanted too but since he want to play with his sweet talk, he was gotta pay. He offered a band and I accepted. He use too panties being thrown at him off his game but he was gonna have to pay for this here pussy. Ya heard me! He wanted to take me to his house in Jersey. I could see the upset in Earl's eyes. I didn't belong to his ugly ass! Niccas are so emotional. I left with Christopher Peterson to avoid checking Earl's ugly feelings in front of his company. I have only one commitment to niccas, I'll keep it moist if they keep it hard. The car ride to Jersey was all small talk. The radio was not helping with an R. Kelly playlist. My hands were sweating, my leg shaking and I had butterflies flutters in my pussy all from anxiousness. I always wanted a piece of Mr. Christopher Peterson. He pulled into the driveway of his house and my anxiety dripped from pussy. He has a very nice house. Indoor Jacuzzi, outdoor pool. But I was impressed with him used a walkie talkie to order a bottle of champagne, ice and glasses from his kitchen to his bedroom. The ceiling in his master bedroom had little glass windows. I

Tuesday, July 4th

laid back and gazed at the stars smiling at me. Christopher Peterson laid back and enjoyed the view with me. We sat up and traded casual conversation about the past and the present. I was inebriated with sexual yearning after drinking one glass full of champagne. I couldn't wait another minute to taste Christopher Peterson's skin. My sexual heat had reached its peak. I pulled the string on his sweat pants and he assisted by going the rest of the undressing. I kneed down between his legs. I embraced his pipe with my right hand. My warm tongue traveled down the shaft. I slowly dragged my tongue to the head. I wrapped my tongue around the head of the pipe as I gently jerked my right hand up and down on the shaft. With the pole covered by the warmth of my mouth my tongue crawled around the head. My warm tongue provoked tears drops of pleasure to double gribble for the eye of the pipe. I pulled my head back and a string of salvia combine with the pipe's dribbles trailed from my lips to eye of the pipe. My pussy cries with anxieties of being pleased. I stand up and stepped out of my thong and squatted on the firm pipe. I lost myself in the moment. I started slowly rolling my watery pussy on the pipe while playing in my weave. Then I bounced my pussy on the firm pipe. My creamy enjoyment splashed onto his balls. The rhythms of my hips made him defensive over his early spill. He slammed his pipe up as I rolled my hips, pressing my pussy down harder onto the firm pipe. His eyes rolled in the back of his head, his mouth wide open, and neck was stuck in between laying down and sitting up position. A few more aggressive roll of my creamy watery pussy and he cummed hard. I could see the veins in his neck popping out. I collect my things and my band. When I turn around to see what Mr. Christopher Peterson was doing. He was sleeping like a baby. I went home with a band and a load of disappointment. Christopher Peterson did have a long dick, definitely above the average 7 inches, but it was skinny, absolutely below the average 5 inches in girth. Who has a half of a big dick? Maybe I'm just greedy. I just expected to be fucked, not to be doing the fucking. It just wasn't a follow up after Mr. Yankee fitted, I'm just saying. Don't get me wrong I did get mines off but it wasn't nothing to be bragging about, mediocre dick. LMAO! Perhaps I should've stuck with my first mind set and fucked Earl's ugly ass. I called my little car service and lucky for me, a driver was in the area. The driver was an Italian wanna bee but was the size a fly. His pomaded hair slicked back, nylon warm-up suit, Saint Anthony gold medallion dangling from his necks with a Jason Giambi's Louisville slugger seated in the passenger's seat, stomach filled with spaghetti, I know cause the sauce stain was on his collar. LOL! He hoped out to open the door for me. I could've batted my eyes and jerked his dick for a ride but just wasn't in the mode to see another sorry looking dick tonight. I had taken a long hot bath and plan to go to bed. It going to be hard to go to sleep with an unsatisfied wet pussy. I know I should be grateful my pockets are full while my pussy starve. GTG!

Wednesday, July 5th

I woke up to summer rain droplets hitting the window pane. The lyrical rain droplets made me warm inside and out. I roll over in my queen size mattress and Gabe is coming in my room with a breakfast tray in his hands. The tray was dressed with two pancakes topped with fresh sliced strawberries and bananas, scrambled eggs, and 4 strips of bacon. Now this was a breakfast with OJ on the side. A little glass vase with 5 flowers made out of 20 dollar bills sticking out on their artificial green stems. Cute a 100 dollar bouquet, literally. Yes I gave Gabe a spare key, don't ask me why? I laid in the bed and ate my breakfast. Gabe decide to put on a movie Love and Basketball, our favorite movie. I guess it reminded us of our situation except I was Omar and Gabe was Sanaa. LMAO! He was upset that he had to find out that I was out of town from my IG. I posted all my favorite pics from my tour with Emery. Gabe, Gabe always whining about something! I was enjoying his quiet conversation until his streamed into the past. TBH we fucked when I 14 yrs old cause Gabe wanted to. I was so wrapped in gear and trying to out do bitches that fucking never crossed my mind. I was getting niccas with head. Why fix what ain't broke? Then I meet Greyson at a high school party in the BX that I went to with Naturel and her running mates. Grayson was 3 years older than me. A trap apartment, driving, Jesus piece swing from solid Cuban link chain and the charm of a hypnotic snake. He had a hold on me, it was like the blood floating through his veins was keeping me alive and feeding my brain. His presence, his touch and his words was keeping me breathing and fueling my emotions. He was like a drug and I was addicted. He fucked me senseless and greasing my pockets. I was living an R&B song while still fucking Gabe. I started lying to Gabe to spend more time with Grayson besides the lies I told to explain the new stuff I was getting. While I lied to Gabe's face his eyes believed I was the good girl he viewed. I was even getting loose by taking pics with Grayson and posting on the book, with the IDC portrayal. Knowing Gabe was trying to be a good man by getting a little part time job trying to feed my greed for fashion. I was so gone and so wrong. To admit insult to injury I started fucking Shady more with my mouth than with my pussy but fucking is fucking right? Shady was a grimy nicca with deep pockets. Bitches was scared of him they fucked him out of fear but I put on like it was my pleasure to fuck him. "A nicca loves a good dick sucker even when the dick ain't in your mouth." is my mom's words, translation from hoe lango is a nicca loves a woman that shows him loving attention. I nicknamed Shady's obese frame, semi-auto cocked eye dipped in midnight blue complexion Big Sexy. He bubbled all over himself every time I said it. LMAO! Then the worst thing happened. I got pregnant. When I told Grayson, this nicca lost it. "I expect some bullshit like this from some ugly bitch trying to trap a nicca but from you, it hurts, what you want more money?" his words was like a shot to my heart without breaking the skin. He stopped the car on the highway and literally dragged me out of his car. And throw 5 hundred dollars on my back as I was pulling myself to my feet. Niccas! He left me on the side of the road with a bloody lip, pregnant and no phone. I had broken my phone and my lip trying to fight my way back in the car. I ended up calling the garage and thank god Louie was working he came and got me after walking a mile to get to a phone. My pride won't let me even tell Shady my condition. I had decided to come clean with Gabe about my dirt. I hit him with the same lame excuse used for the list I posted. I wasn't cheating I was experimenting. I was just mouth fucking them niccas, it was just business, I was gonna get right back. To be spotless I had to shed all the filth. This was hardest thing I ever had to do, snatching on my own self. Staring into Gabe's pretty brown eyes I felt ashamed of me. But Gabe pushed away from me the hurt in his eyes leaked with pain when I needed him to comfort me for my self-inflicted wounds. His pain cut my heart. In that very moment I wished that I could've turn back the hands of time and erase everything that was poking at Gabe's heart but time wasn't in my hands but Gabe's pain was. I wanted to eat the words I spit in the air. But I was tired of hiding me. I love to fuck, if I get paid off it then better for me! So I freed my soul of secrets I told Gabe I pregnant, it wasn't his and I was going to get AB. The words was easy to say hard as hell to do. The AB clinic ain't no joke. There RL protesters. "7 women died on the table up there!" "It's a human life you killing!" their words shot down my spine. The posters of little tiny hands and feet poking out of a glob of blood made my stomach flip upside down and I throw up on my new sneakers. Naturel said don't give them no eye contact and keep walking. Inside was ever more scary than the protesters. The last thing I saw were tubes and doctors masked faces while laying on gurney and then I awake up to me sitting in a chair with a nurse shoving hot tea and hospital cracker packs in my face. After everything was sad and done I had killer camps in my stomach and in my heart. At the two week checkup I found out Greyson didn't only give me a baby but a shot in the ass, curable STD. That raw special feeling that he was giving me, he was just giving to somebody else. As my body healed so did my mind. I needed to be alone free to roam. And I wasn't bitter from the sex-perience, honestly. I enjoy the facial expression of men or niccas when they are in superb pussy. It's a pleasure to have a men or nicca to hit the right spot at the right time. I love sucking hardcore street thugs dicks keeping them on their toes turning them into Ballerinas with my mouth. Sex in the air is aroma therapy for me. LMAO. I massage words and skin so niccas feel it and many are willing to pay for it! RT "You can't go around playing with people's feelings and except to keep getting away with it." Is Gabe's prediction. I play with nicca's body and words for amusement. They play with their own feelings. It's an even exchanged sex for money or dick for pussy, depending on how I'm felling. Niccas be knowing what it is but think they "that nicca" that's going to change the game. Play by the rules of the game and nobody gets hurt. I'm a pro, so I get paid for my game. Isn't that the way it goes in any sport? LOL! "I'm so into you no one else will do." Is what he said. His words had my eyes more gloomy then weather outside the window. I have love for Gabe but not his type of his love. He wants to cuff me to his hip. Fuck ooout of here! It still hurts to see him in a fog of pain. I showered him with some of my creamy rain. My tender kisses washed away his pain for the moment. I could see the sunshine in his face as his thunder strive. As he slashed inside and out my creamy puddles. The banging of my headboard made it pour creamy rain all over his thunder strives. We fucked like rabbits until we fell asleep, completely washed out. As I nap I could feel Gabe kissing me in my sleep, whispering "I love you's" in my ear. I wanted to check him while we were fucking for playing the "who pussy is it?" game. I let him rock since he was feeling bad and shit but now he was just trying to chill too hard. He want me to paint a rainbow filled with a storm of windy lies. Giving him what he wanted would be not only lying to him but to myself. But when I open my eyes Gabe was gone. I could still feel his kisses on my skin even though he was gone. I could still hear his voice and laughter in the air, his scent still in the atmosphere. Gabe is the "right" type of man, just not for me. I laid in the bed a little longer to enjoy the sweet lyrical rain droplets on the window as my pussy hummed along. I got up out the bed and washed way Gabe's overcast of emotions. By the time I came out the shower the sun was shining bright like the summer rain had never happened, expect for the damp ground the only clue of the summer rain. The weather matched me and Gabe. I was going on with my day like he was never here, expect for the damp spots on the sheets was the only clue of Gabe's presences. I had decided to run thru my hood, which meant visit my mom's crib. I dolled up but not club dolled up. I packed my sex-tra lashes. I took a pic and posted on IG for my WCW. People can say what they want about me I love me. I so comfortable in my skin it crazy. What can I say "I feeling myself" LOL! A stop in the hood always meant I would check up Mr. Buster and holler at grease monkey Louie. And of course I had to remind Earl our friendship is in a no flex zone. That attitude shit he pulled the other night when I slid off with Christopher Peterson was unacceptable and will not be tolerated. I will fuck who I want to and charge them or nah, my choice. LOL! He asked me not to pick up niccas in his face out of respect for our friendship, I agreed. Earl wanted to fuck but he was on punishment for his behavior. So I choked on his loud and I breezed to my moms crib. Kayla's 7th birthday is next Saturday. The little girl has an obsession with circuses. Any and every time I've offered to take her anywhere in NYC her hearts desires, she always scream "the circus." And I always comply. We have been too them all 2 times. So for her birthday I rented space in central park for 12 hundred, a tent and set up crew for a stack, an animal trainer with a monkey, a clown, a DJ and a magician in one, a face painting artist and a fucking pony. I rented a cotton candy machine, a snow cones machine and a picture taking booth. I ordered more than enough burgers, hotdogs and 30 pizza which are her all favorite foods. All her friends were invited. I spent a grip so she could get loose. I hope she enjoys herself. The last thing I had to do was pay the last part on the cake shape like a balloons which I took care of today. When I walked thru the door both of my little sisters were running toward me, Gia and Kayla. Gia lives in Russia with our father. My father took a gymnastic trainer position years ago at a private school, Kindergarten thru high school. A free roof over his head, a salary and a free education for Gia. The school had one spot available, when the job was offered. Gia fit the age spot and she had the blood stain of our moms. We all could've went but my moms was fucking some nicca on the side and couldn't stand to leave him but gave the excuse of not being able to stomach me and Goldie being giving an inferior education, BS!!! So my father packed up Gia and bounce and never looked back. Niccas! Gia always comes home around Kayla's birthday and send a week with us and then return to her flips and ribbons. Of course my moms took Gia's visit as an in house baby sitter and was gone most of the time. I chilled for a minute. Me and Gia traded phone so we could go though each other pictures, its our way of catching up. Think about it if you really want to know about a person look through their camera roll. The caption of someone's life moments are in a picture. I'm going straight from the hood to work. BRB!!!

Thursday, July 6th

Last night was my 1st day back to work after my mini vac. Black was going extra hard about his little medical form. FOH! My appointment is in 3 weeks. Could you believe he wanted to see my appointment slip. Like WTF! Who lies about a doctor appointments? From his attitude I could tell, him and Naturel were on bad terms. As for as my coins for the night, I did okay. I've seen better Wednesdays but a 2 band and a half any nothing to be looking down on. The LMS boos came out to show love, they really miss me, aww! LOL! The LMS, like my status nicca. These are niccas that I've never met and it if I did they just didn't qualify to get this here pussy. But you know your gurl don't discriminate, money is green no matter what color the hand it comes from. I turned up with drink on deck and molly flowing thru my body. You know a nicca just had to over step with his hands and Jah black ass had to check him. The BS that comes with the fucking club. After work at like 4 in the morning I had a taste chicken and waffle, so I had the driver of the night, some clown I didn't even listen for his name, take me uptown to the chicken and waffle house. I was looking thru the pics I stole from Gia's phone yesterday. LOL! I post a pic of the whole family together for TBT. The picture captured our last Christmas morning as a family. Goldie was 14 yrs old, I was 12 yrs old and Gia 10 yrs old. We under the Christmas tree ravage thru the gifts looking for our name with cold in our eyes and heat in our breath, LOL. My father sitting in his king reclining leather chair with a smile on his face and a cup of coffee in his hand. Our excitement showed he had done his job. My moms is in the picture mouth wide open and tears streaming from the diamond bracelet uncovered as her Christmas gift. The picture was taken by my father's new camera with a set timer that we picked out with our moms. The old days when we were all under one roof. Of course we got on each other's nerves but the love was real. I sat at a high table for 2 like 10 feet away from the door. I like people watching, people are hilarious. After 10 minutes of me eating a squad of hood niccas walked in the restaurant. Nicca comes in all flavors. A hood nicca has no regards for real life consequences. The type of nicca who shoots another person and is surprised when he goes to jail. But one nicca stood out, he had on the hood nicca attire but he didn't move like a hood nicca. We noticed each other at the same time. It was an instant attraction for me. His dark caesar, with the money Mitch half-moon part, evenly spread dark chocolate skin, with a plaid button up and khaki cargo shorts. What was driving me sexual insane was the jingle of shoelace's metal hoop on his $\frac{3}{4}$ beef and broccoli colored tims. Every time he took a step that jingle was vibrating my pussy. He walked over to me, propped his elbow on the table as he leaned in close to me to speak but his scent of Calvin Klein's euphoria spoke ecstasy. "What a pretty young thang is going out here this time of the morning?" his voice was so deep it echoed in my panties. His sent had my pussy floating in bliss to the point I was smiling senseless, looking completely insane. It was a ridiculous sight I know. He asked for my number twice not cause I didn't hear him but cause I was sitting there looking fucking stupid like a star struck juvenile, grinning. TBH, I was blinded by his chocolate sexiness, fondled by the jingle singing from his boots, the ecstasy pouring off of him pierced my nose and excited my taste buds. I wanted to drink his babies. He pleaded for my number but it was displayed in a nonchalant tone. He wasn't too proud to beg and neither was I. The hood niccas that were with him called his name

Thursday, July 6th

"Bengee". When he turned his body to respond to them I was gone. I didn't take his number cause I didn't trust my pussy so I packed up my uneaten food and left him my number written in lipstick on a napkin. I decided to go home and take a nap before I start pussy dialing on my phone. That Bengee really make my pussy pulsate. I got up around 3 in the afternoon from my nap. I had to meet up with Naturel at Ivory's house. Ivory's birthday is on the 28th of this month. I always feel awkward round Ivory. I'm just use to seeing her move like I move not glued to a motor chair with her lifeless leg leaning to the side. She joked about it "At least I'll never wear out my favorite shoes or sneaker" shit like that just wasn't funny to me. We settled on a high school theme. Naturel job is to drum up the food and decorations. My job is to find a spot. I already had the perfect spot in mind. I love Ivory like a sister but once the plans were settle my skin was crawling to get out of there. Anything and everything I say just seems like the wrong thing to say. What do you say to a person who lost their leg by the hands of a nicca you love? It's a demoralize situation on so many different levels. My heart bleeds for her. Then I got a text from a strange number. It's recruiting season. I've passed my number to many niccas. I just wait to see who call. LMAO! Then I weed through to see who might be a keep for the cuffing season. LOL! It could've been absolutely anybody texting me but my pussy was hoping it was Bengee. Whoever it was they had to refresh my memory. When the image filled my screen my pussy started whistling at the past reflection of the imprint reviled by the white linen suit at the Emery's 4th of July party. Eyebrows like plush velvet over sliced almond shaped eyes, long seductive eye lashes, a quarter size brown mole on his left cheek looked like a chocolate chip. The complexion of a perfectly baked cookie, not too dark and not too light, I wanted to bite him and see how the cookie crumb. LMAO! Chocolate chip cookies has always been my comfort food. After scheduling to meet up in about an hour at pink berry on 2nd ave. I politely breezed on Ivory and Naturel. The ride down 2nd ave. I was hoping Chocolate chip cookie don't crush under pussy pressure. You won't believe how many bitch niccas has failed under pussy pressure. Ode lame excuses "I got a girl" ok and? Or the bougie type that's selective with where they pull their dick out. Brah please!

Thursday, July 6th

Nicca this here is just some pussy nobody asking for a ring or trying to trap your bitch ass. A lot of niccas talk a good one but when this pussy on their neck they collapse to a bitch nicca. I arrived to the meeting ground before he did. I was set up a table in the corner. My pussy wanted me to text him, looking thirsty, but mind just chilled. I wasn't jacking me being stood up. The about 6 feet even in height something like 50 cent wide chocolate chip cookie fell thru the restaurant's doors. The visible imprint in front of his jeans informed my pussy of his arrival. He greeted me with a kiss on the cheek before going to the counter to get himself a smoothie. He sat down across from me. Looking at his face I noticed the speckled chocolate chips on his skin. I decided Chipy would be his nick name. The suggestive chocolate chips wanted tasting. His confident eyes stared at my hard allusive nipples poking out from under the thin sun dress. He sitting here disclosing his relationship BI. After a 4 years his girl left him, with no clue or warning. I wanted his full acknowledgement of their sex life. A bitch will only bounce without looking back after 4 years if that dick ain't right. LOL! He didn't have any complaints but no compliments either from his point of view. At 1st I was annoyed that he wanted to discuss his past relationship. From my outfit and the way I was talking I was screaming DTF not Oprah or Dr. Oz. FOH! He was still having confessional. SMFH! He never had frozen yogurt or an open convo about sex. He complained that his hands were cold but body was hot. I told him between my legs was steaming hot and icy cold, he could warm his fingers and cool his body. He accepted my offer and added his own submission of fingers gliding in and out of my panty less pussy under the table. His fingertip were gentle and soft in my pussy and in my mouth. I sucked my cream of his fingers. The act provoked our sexual desires. We ended up in the back seat of his Escalade, sundress on the car floor. His lips scaled my skin from my neck to my navel. His sculpted body was magnetic to my hands and lips. I caressed him with my hands and lips, kissing and touching each chocolate chips embedded in his sweet skin covering his chest. Then he mounted by body. He inserted his dick and I almost jumped out of my skin. His mouth spoke in a raunchy tone, "Lie back and take this dick." His words of threaten ecstasy made my pussy quiver with wel-cumming anticipation. His dick was the equivalent to a Pillsbury cookie dough roll. My pussy walls strengthen while under attack of the cookie dough. After a few trundles my pussy's walls adjusted. Yes his cookie dough was hitting my ribs but my ribs wanted to beat like a drum. I put my right leg on his left shoulder and held my left leg to the side. I cleared his path so he could get deep in this creamy buttered pussy and I shouted words of encouragement. "DON'T SLOW DOWN! GET IN THIS PUSSY" We eye witnessed the cookie dough kneeling the insides of my pussy. My creamy pleasure overflowed into his pubic hairs and dripped down on to the leather seats. I was walking on the car ceiling shouting more instructions, "PUSH HARDER, FASTER, ALMOST THERE, DEEPER" The clangs of his balls on leather seat sounded like smacking lips on delicious sweet treat. His hand were planted on backside of my tights. The heat of the moment had the car tinted window sweating. My gluttonous pussy sounded for pleasure as he explode with creamy enjoyment. His mouth chimes with the crumbles of the cookie dough. After we fuck he offered to drive me home. I accepted the offer but had him drop me off at my moms crib didn't want a Monty repeat. LOL! Monty bitch ass! On the drive he question his performance. I keep it sex-tra moist and told the truth. He had the tool but didn't know how to use it. He has the potential to leave me pigeon toed or even crawling. But he didn't know how to handle his tool. I offered to teach him. It may only take 4 lesson for a band a lesson. He wanted to think about it. I wondered did I offend him? I was trying to help him! Unless he meet a patient woman. She'll take her time and teach him how to fuck, otherwise women going to keep jumping ship until he learn to swim. From my moms crib I call my car service to take me home. In the ride and in the shower my mind was stuck on the idea of a school for sex. an institution that teach women to suck dick properly, teach men eat pussy, teach women how front on little dick and take big dick, teach men how to fuck all pussy adequately. What you think of a school of sex? FOH!! Niccas ain't ready for that and I'll be out of a job. LOL! Well I going to take a nap before work! BRB

Other Thursday night at work was no different from any night I eating while bitches were watching and starving. They was giving and getting attitude. Like FOH! If you don't like you job go cashier. Like for real!! one of them hoes told Black I was cutting throat. FOH!!! My LMS niccas come to the club checking for me from my IG pics! My cliental up! LOL! Hating ass bitches! After work I grab something to eat and went straight to Louie and checked up Mr. Buster. I need some shop therapy. I was still a little hot from last night. Bitch was like I only make so much in tip cause I be fucking niccas. No bitches I get tip cause I know how to work my lips and I'm not taking about my pussy lips either. I be word fucking these nicca! I know what type of man needs to feel which words to soften his pockets. I do sale conversation with my pussy lips but that after work hours. Why they mad? LMAO! At like 7 pm I get a text from Westley Brooks. The drop on West, he's bout 5'8, a light beard, and shoulder length dreads. I'm not one for dreads but his were well care for. They are neat, shiny, and thin. He was well in to 40's with no gray hairs and didn't look a day over 30 years old. The most attractive feature of West is he is a black man. City job, wife, 2.5 kids, white picketed fence living the American dream. The only hole in his life is his wife don't give him head. See this is a perfect example of how a woman could lose a good man. West wife pulled out all the freak spot on the way to wedding but once she got her man she only rides downtown on birthday and anniversaries. Women think cause they got a man they don't have to compete. Everything you won't do I will do for the right price. LOL. Sucking dick is a skill. Bitches be acting like they scared to touch the dick. Or they be acting shy don't want a nicca to watch, hiding under covers and shit. It's only skin. Not me! When I'm toping a nicca off, I go in, LMAO! West will text me like once a months with a location and a time. I'll meet him there and we'll find a spot so he could get his nut off and I could be compensated for my services. I didn't consider what I was doing to West as cheating. And this is where me and Gabe can't see eye to eye on this topic. Cheating to me is building an emotional bond with a person. Fucking is pure physical, like a contact sport. So I meet West at a small little restaurant slash bar on west 23rd street. We had small convo like the weather bullshit, words with no meaning

Friday, July 7th

floating in the air. He excused himself and headed for the men's restroom. I waited for the guy that I saw go in before West to exit the restroom and I went for it. If there was another men in there I planned to play drunk and excuse myself. But I was lucky, West was in restroom alone. I jimmied the restroom door with my scrunchie that was on my right waist. I back West up against the wall. I tugged at his belt on his slacks. Once his zipper on his slacks was open I reached inside his briefs and gentle massage his man cake with my right hand my fingers jingle his sugar knots. I leaned in close to his body. My titis were in his face as I whispered in his ear "Where you wanna cum at today? I'm going to suck the cum out your dick." the words harden his man cake and tighten his sugar knots. I slide down his frame into a squat position. I brought down his slacks and briefs along with my body. His slack and brief were rings around his ankles. I used my right hand to stroke his shaft and my left hand keep the knots warm. My lips followed the lead of my right hand. Gently and slowly I drag my lips up and down the shaft. I stick my tongue out to taste the sugar knots while I ate the man cake. Fast and rough I pulled my lips up the shaft to the bottom of the head. I caressed the head to tip with my tongue. I pull the cake out my mouth as my hand grazed the skin on the shaft. I released some spittle on the tip and spread the wetness on the cake and knots. I deep throated the cake continuously. My lips glided up and down the cake relentlessly at rapid speed. A whole lot of spit, til it dripped. He stood on his toes like a prima ballerina praising the lord "OH, Thank god" he shouted. I could taste the custard beginning to squirt for the cake. My lips gripped hard and my head bounced harder. West gave me 7 hundred dollars. I had him believing that by me helping him he was helping me with rent. LMAO. Even if his wife start sucking dick tomorrow it will be years before she could even look at me much less compete. LMAO! West had me horny and shit I wanted to fuck but needed to nap before work. I took my frustrated pussy home. Ugh! Horny.com! GTG

Friday, July 7th

Saturday, July 8th

Last night was the night of niccas just trying the shit out of me, I was so mad I wanted to catch a body. I'm coming of my brownstone to get in to my car for the night, an icy snow white X5, and guess who is whining on the right side of the car, you guessed it bitch ass Monty. Brah!!! Get your shit together! I do admit this here is some awesome pussy but Brah! Every Friday night I guess the wife lets him out to play and he come stalking. Last night was going to be his last night of this BS. I told him I had his wife number and I pulled it up on my phone to show his bitch ass it wasn't a game. No means No. FOH! Clowns! I think he got the picture but to make sure I took a picture of his dunk ass and sent the picture along with his job and home address to Tank's drop phone. These hoes ain't loyal!!! Aye! If his girl only knew he was out here begging to suck on my pussy with the same lips he kiss her goodnight with. SMFH! I bet he'll regret running his mouth to Jah black ass, after we fucked that one time, I repeat that one time. The club wasn't jumping like a winter Friday night. See the summer time money is good money for the club scene. That why I've been hollering at Naturel for the plug in at her night club. Niccas will pay to see ass in

Saturday, July 8th

the winter cause bitches is covered up outside but in the summer all bitch, females and women are all fucking naked. Naturel is a host and she gets a band a night. I wanted the feature spot. Its once a week for 2 bands. And other bitch be getting the feature off of number of followers on IG, I'm up to 500k. But bitches be acting funny, I think she wants me to stay at the club to keep an eye on Black nasty ass. FOH! I ain't nobody's dick watcher. What if I started acting funny and put her ass out but I don't get down like that yet. LOL! For a Friday night I made $270 on my pay check and $1750 in tips. As I was leaving the club Jah run down on me, talking bout he got his money up and he wanted to pay to play. Like I say it was showtime at Apollo type of nicca night, any clown can take the stage. Ok I had a performance for his ass. LOL. We agreed to meet at the hotel in the BX. His thirsty ass had already checked in and had the key card to the room in his hand, when I walked up to the hotel entrance. A regular nicca would've at least waited in the room. This nicca is a fucking dub. As we walked down the hallway to the elevator to take it to the 2nd floor I could see the anxiousness in Jah's eyes it felt slimy. We got in the room and he jump out of his clothes. His body was everywhere and nowhere all at the same time. His hard 4x4 dick was drowning in wild pubic hair. I took of my dress and kept my underwear on. He flopped down on bed. I saw the pint of henny on the night stand on his side. I offered to pour us a shot. I laid down on my side. He poured us a 2nd shot of henny. He gulped down 3 shot back to back. He wasted no time and stared pawing at me breast tugging at my bra, no finesse or style just a brut. He consumed my nipples like a malnourished infant. His excited hunger caused him to start taking small bit of my nipple. It wasn't sexy it was creepy. He licked on my pussy but I didn't get no enjoyment from his tongue on my skin. It felt slimy. He licked my pussy like a dog drinking water. I told him my contacts were bothering my eyes I went to the bathroom and I came out completely naked. With the Visine in my hand. I went and pour us shot of henny each. With his eye glued to my ass I dropped 4 drops of Visine in his shot. I laid on flabby chest and played in his forests of hair on his chest. Within minutes he was completely out. His snoring was brain wreaking. I used my empty shot glass to mix baby powder and water together. The mixed made a nice paste. I rubbed some of the paste on Jah's dick and pour the rest in a side an unused condom. I put the condom in the toilet. I took my pay out of Jah's pocket. When Jah wakes up he'll have the chalky residue on dick and condom in the toilet all the evidence will lead to him believing that he fucked the shit out of me. LOL! I got home like 5 this morning. I showered from the thought of Jah dirty fingernail's pawing at my skin. Ewe! I try to sleep the image out of my sight. I woke up at like one in the afternoon. I got dressed and put my game face on. Kayla birthday party in Central Park was going to be some shit. here's the drop, Kayla's and Taylor's father, Monroe had left my moms for my older sister Goldie, who is now 6 months pregnant by Monroe. My maternal Grandmother had an old bone with my moms for marrying my father at 19 yrs olds and throwing away her gymnastics career. My moms's only sister, Free, short for Freedom, had an ongoing achievement competition going on with my moms. Me and Gia didn't really talk to Goldie after she shitted on our moms. Goldie is a heartless bitch. I wanted to ask her one question... Are you raising your child with the knowledge that their half-sister and brother are also his/her aunt and uncle?

I'm a believer but I'm not into the religion thing at all but for Goldie there is definitely a hell waiting on her. I'm glad I suggested a public place people will be force to pretend to be civilized. I wore an oversized football jersey that I got altered to my size to fit like a dress with a pair of dunks on my feet. This the match of all the families "uglies". I didn't know if I was going to break up a fight or get in one myself. But everybody stayed in their corner. Free had 3 sons same age as me, Goldie and Gia. Darren, Daniel, and Denzel they were cool cousins but square and pointy, LMAO. I was the host so I walked around with a fake smile on my face being fake nice. Under the red and yellow tent was an animal trainer with a monkey, a clown, a DJ and a magician, a face painting artist and a fucking pony, a cotton candy machine, a snow cones machine and a picture taking booth, more than enough burgers, hotdogs and 30 pizza which are Kayla's favorite things. Everyone had a smile which gave a smile. My moms sent me and Earl back to house to pick up the ice cream cake. Earl's loud head ass need to blow. So went to his house 1st to blow it down and Earl really thought it was a game. I dead ass put him on punishment. He couldn't have any of this pussy.

Saturday, July 8th

Earl's ugly ass pushed me up against the wall. I pretend like I was pushed him off me. His newfound aggression was explosive in my panties. He pinned me up against the wall in his room. He bent down in front of me, forcing his ugly face under my dress. I pushed his head away when I wanted to pull his face closer. My resistance made Earl fight harder to get my juices on his tongue. His hostility charged with sexual desire was a new look on Earl's passive skin. He popped my G-string with his teeth only the elastic around my waist was still intact. His sexual potency was liquefying. He aggressively pushed my play fighting hands to the side. He lift me up me on his shoulders like an untamed beast. With my tights resting on his shoulder I could see every muscle in Earl's ugly arms flexing. From our play wrestling his arms glanced. My legs were hanging over his shoulder while his face was buried between my legs. He used his hands to grip each one of my ass cheek to hold me in position while his tongue sting at my soul. My back was up against the wall with my palms planted on the ceiling. His tongue violently fondle the opening of my pussy. His lips slurped on my clit. The sound drove my pussy to creamy tears. I used both of my hands to palm the top of his head to brace for the ultimate orgasm. I was startled by the loud moan of pleasure escaping my lips. I closed my eyes. It felt like the universe was spinning. He laid me down on his bed with his tongue latched on to my clit. He had my legs spread open across the bed. His hands gripped the inside of my tights. I creamed on his tongue so hard it arched my back and my hands gripped the sheets. He walked up the bed on his knuckles like with King Kong. He placed his left hands on the top of his head broad. He splattered in my puddles of delight with his monster dick guided by his right hand. My body quivered with pain and pleasure. He grabbed the inside of my tights. The monsters head was pounding on my chest bones. Earl's monster was punishing me for reprimanding Earl. The sturdy pounding turned into thumping, then turned into fist pounding body blows. I placed my hands on the front of his tights to lighten the blows but my hands was weak from the combination of pain and pleasure. The collision inside my body spilled out onto the monster's head. Just when I thought the end was near the monster grasped a second gulp of air. The drumming on ribs vibrated through my body. Sweat dripped from his forehead like my cream dripped on the monster. The monster's tempo dance in my creamy walls was a new melody. My slippery walls were closing in on the pulsating monster. The squeezing surroundings triggered the creamy flow of moans from the monster. Earl is usually a gentle ride and when he is on the verge of cumming the ride gets bumpy. I could take the bumps cause it was near the end of the ride but today the ride was hell from begin to end. Earl ugly ass had quality dick. I wanted to bounce on Earl's ugly ass right after but my legs were weaker than cooked noodles, I barely could move my legs. I'm completely against pillow talking but I had to tell Earl about Jah thirsty ass. We shared a good laugh at Jah's expense, literally LMAO! Earl fucked like a Trey Songz's album but looked like a Rich Gang remix. After fucking Earl I needed to take a nap it was no way in hell I would be able to dance on anybody's stage without a little shut eye. So I went back to the park after bushing down my weave the best way I could with water and my hands, sang happy birthday silently and jumped in a gapsy cab, yup I sure did. I didn't have the patience or the leg power to be standing around waiting on a service car. I didn't care what the

Saturday, July 8th

"family" had to say about how, what or why I left. Getting inside my home was like seeing heaven. I just took a nice hot bath. I got 2 hours and 20 minutes to nap before work. So TTYL!

Sunday, July 9th

Last the club was popping! The drop on Bengee, so I met him 3 days ago at the chicken and waffle spot, remember? Well since that day he's been sending little thought full text. Like "good morning beautiful." or "just texting see if you made it home alright." I know you saying what's the big deal but it's was major to me. Bengee is a sexy black god but had nicca in him. Any way he offered to treat me to breakfast after work. I agreed. I'm usually the 1st dancer out the door at 3:15 when the club close at 3. I didn't mingle with my co-workers after hours. They were plain ole messy. Security sleeping with dancers, dancers steeling from each other. Just shit I didn't have time for. My money was what I went to work to get and that's all I took out of there. But this morning it was 3:34 and I was still standing outside the club. I wasn't alone. Sugar thinks she top bitch cause she fucking Black's nasty ass. Apparently she try to flex her weight on Cinnamon. Now Cinnamon been down for Black for quite some time. Sugar was up in Cinnamon's face. Cinnamon had that look in her eye like "bitch I'm about to wash your dirty ass" when black came outside and end the whole show. Mind you not to long ago they were BFFs. Bitches will turn on you faster than a nicca but slower than family. Jah going to bring his goofy doofy ass over to me. I can't help but laugh at him every time I see him! I really zoed this dumb nicca! LMAO! He asking do I need a ride? Braaaah! I would walk from here to Africa before I get a ride to my home from you! And thanks to your 15 hundred I can take a cab better yet buy a little pit pit like you driving! FOH clown! I could see his little feeling was hurt but was I wrong? If you buy a bag, jewelry or shoes, every time you see the owner of the business you expect him/her to be snubbing you nose? No! and I'm not doing it either. Niccas drop them coins and I lift up my skirt. Same game I been running since the 5th grade. Aye! LMAO! Finally Bengee showed up in a bright blue 525i BMW. It a very nice car but its just tight. I like cars that I can move around in. What if I wanted to top him off? I'm just saying. He wanted to go to After Midnight. After Midnight is out of the hood but close enough that hood niccas could get to it. His intention was pure. He was think since we were in BK he was doing something by taking me to Manhattan. At that time of the morning there was no traffic. He has 3 kids with 3 different woman. He has legal custody of 2, boys 15 and 13. The 8 yrs old girl lives with her moms. He gets his time with the daughter every other weekend. A nicca turn Black man but in society's view "once a nicca always a nicca." but he is still fight the system as a Black man. Currently single, renting an apartment, and working at scaffolding company. And is a huge R&B fan. He was playing some panty wetters. It was something about him. Every time I'm around him I turn in to this shy little puppy. I sat and grinned. When we got to the restaurant it was showtime at the Apollo part 2. Jah and more clowns from the block was at After Midnights. I walked right by Jah silly ass while he trying to speak. Niccas just don't respect the curve!! We work at the same fucking club, we saw each other all night. Why the fuck do I gotta acknowledge you? FOH! I couldn't believe Jah try to flex and grab my arm and demand a hello. Out of nowhere Bengee stretched Jah out. Jah words "Thanks for the pussy" got him what he deserve, to be knocked out. Bengee grab my hand and we jumped back into his car. His hand started swelling. It was more convenient to go to his apartment on 120th and 5th ave. What stood out in his amazing 3 bedroom apartment was the balcony and the mirrors on the ceiling in his bedroom. Something touch my heart when he showed me his daughter's room. It had all the trimmings for a princess it was beautiful. The room matched his feelings. His daughter is his queen. He was her faithful servant and that melted my heart. He wrapped his hand with an ice pack and begun cooking breakfast. His lips never stop moving. I was grateful he was doing all the talking I didn't have to explain Jah's words or my pussy's mileage before he pulled up into my life. The down side is because he didn't act on Jah's words and go for the score I couldn't ask to play. Fucking Jah! He filled me in on the personalities of his children. Hilarious stories of playfulness, love and loyalty. From the words of memory jumping from his mouth he wasn't just a father he was a Daddy and he enjoyed it. He wished he had pick different woman to have his kids withbut he had accepted his errors in life as lessons. He was a positive Black man with some sprinkles of a nicca but not the average nicca. I sat there like a little kid hanging on to every word, laughing to tears squirt from my eyes, just enjoying his presence. It feel like I was hypnotized. This was the 1st man that could actually hold a conversation with

Sunday, July 9th

me and not have sex in his eyes and not see sex in my eyes. When I see a nicca or black man I see dick or money nothing more and nothing less. But looking at Bengee I saw something and felt something more. We talked as he cooked breakfast. He then invited me to his son's baseball game. I wanted to say yes but I was just wore out from dancing all night. I just wanted to fuck and go home. But I couldn't bring myself to straight up ask Bengee for the dick, especially after Jah's words. It was like the words were on the tip of my tongue but wouldn't leave my lips. I know my pussy was mad at me for this one but I declined with a hug goodbye. He try to drive me home but y'all already know how I feel about a nicca knowing where I live at, hell to the no no!! Thank you Monty for that lesson. I took a shower to wash away Jah's words and take a nap to rest my crying pussy. I planned to find a nicca to fuck me unconsciously to get Bengee out my senses. I found myself spontaneous laugh at one of Bengee jokes from earlier. I was slipping and falling into Bengee. WTF!!! I really needed a nap. I woke up in the late afternoon. My pussy was purring but my legs didn't want to do the foot work to get some dick. So I lounged around

Sunday, July 9th

the house before getting ready for work while my mind ran around Bengee. I'll get some dick after work to get me away from the Bengee fairy tale and back to reality! LMAO!

Finally Mohammad was back! He was out due to back problems. I was so happy to see him, jerking his curry dick with a little spit was no problem. Last night was a dud at the club! UGH! A squad of seniors raided the club, a few of my LMS boos came thru. I took the stage like a professional and collected my ones. I even had a few private dances. A band on a hot Sunday summer night that was doing great. LOL! My pussy was snap, crackling and popping it need to be milked. I had Mohammad drive me to the meat packing district of Manhattan to Sweet Watah lounge. The lounge has soft red lighting. Plush red couches lined the walls under the soaring granite arches of a Catalan vaulted tiled ceiling, giving the atmosphere a luxury sexy vampire lair feel. Perfect for me cause I was hoping to feed on some flesh tonight. LMAO!! This spot is always jumping but it was dead last night. I was sexually frustrated so I throw in the towel and called it a night. Showered and shut it. I didn't sleep good. It's hard to sleep with my pussy growling thru the night. But I know my 3pm appointment with my MCM will make quiet my pussy for a little while. Marcus Lumar is a chocolate gladiator, sexy delicious eye candy. I have only missed one appointment since training started one year ago. And I only missed that one cause I was in LA last week remember? Besides the fact that I liked when my eyes drooled over him, he's actually a great unconventional trainer. He used New York City as his gym. I loved the adventure of it. The text at 2:30 with the location. Like a secret mission. LOL! Today we going to meet at 155th and Bradhurst. Marcus always begins with a stretch. This the part where we brush up against each other. And I'm reminded why Marcus is good to look at and nothing else, no dick. LML! Today's fitness goal was 2 rounds, up and down the 102 stairs, then I did 50 upside down sit up on a playground monkey bars. Then the post stretch. I took a picture of Marcus pouring water over his overheated body and posted my MCM! I hailed a cab in the street! Yup cause it was fucking 90 degrees outside and after the workout it felt like 200 and since I haven't been fucked in 52 hours I was hot in more ways than one. OMG! The thirst be so real! Once in my brownstone I took a shower I was going to spend some one on one time with Gia. I called my car service I needed a driver for the day and I needed it to be Mohammad. Of course Nicholas ass showed up, Mohammad back was out again. UGH!!! He picked me up at my brownstone then we went to my moms crib to scoop Gia. We went to Spring Street to shop. I bought her some clothes at Hollister, 2 good down coats at Patagonia, Russia is fucking freezing, 2 pair of ugg boots, and sister matching bracelets and Pandora, it was extra for the trinkets. I spent half of 10 stacks from Emery. We were hungry so we grabbed burgers at mickey d's. Tonight Gia will be on a plane back to Russia and I won't get to see her in person until next summer. Yeah we keep up with each other thru face time and all but the love that's there is not felt. Gia is the youngest but the wisest. She is 19 yrs old now. 3 time gymnastic gold medalist and a virgin. But had her eye on a young man named Aldrich. He is currently training with her. I didn't ask about my father she just volunteered it. She joked that he was just like me a sexoholic. I laughed her off and changed the subject. We talked about Goldie's mannerisms at the Kayla's birthday party with her nose in the air acting like she was breaking her lips to speak, with Monroe's bitch ass hanging from her pussy lips like a piercing. How do bitches that are in the wrong have the rights to an attitude? Like somebody did something to her? Gia noticed that Goldie was grilling our moms while she was taking the family pics with Monroe and the kids. I didn't peep. Goldie is soooo sherm! She can have any nicca men or whatever but she had to have her moms's man. WOW! I know 1st hand that when that pussy get that thirst, shit gets real but to fuck and keep is wrong in its self and to add the icing on the cake it's your moms's man! Goldie! SMFH! On our way out of mickey d's I walked straight into a blossoming tender bone. Full grown tender bones has prefect gentleman posture, confidence, excellent bedroom skills and stunning looks. The type of looks that snatch the eyes of every lady and womEn that set on him. This here wasn't full grown he was on the cusp of it. I only gave him a few minutes to impress me for my number because he caught my phone that he knocked out of my hand accidently when we walked into each other literally. He was dressed like an average nicca, with an average job, probably driving dick on average stick, spiting that average shit. I love them younguns that think they can fuck with this. I get a kick out of shoving them around with this above average pussy. He won my number with that baby face and his confidence.

Monday, July 10th

I can't wait to bust Tyree open like a dutch, I'm going to learns him. LMAO! We hooped back in the car, we were on our way to the airport to drop Gia off. When I picked her up from my moms crib we loaded up the back of the Surban with her suitcase. I saw my father standing at the entrance waiting on Gia thru the car tinted window I didn't even get out the car. I usually send Gia in the car by herself to avoid this view. I really need a drink and some dick, but my phone wasn't popping, on this Monday night. Finally a text from Chipy. He was a $100 short of a band, my mind didn't like that plan but my pussy wanted to understand. We met at the hotel. I whipped this pussy on him while tutoring him on how to kneel his cookie dough. HA!! Scrumptious late night treat. LMAO! My car service was waiting on me downstairs. I timed it perfectly, fun money. I'm home now just watching TV pussy still purring. TTYL!

I woke up to the smell of cooked beacon in the air. I got out of bed and it was Naturel all chirpier, chef cooking with the pot. Aye! Her and Black are back together and she is moving back in with him. Whatever! If he kicks her out in 3 months again then the couch will be waiting for her. SMFH! And she's inviting me to a "Ladies night out" on Thursday night. We ate, sipped and talked. At around noon I start getting ready today. I was going to the heights to met up with Julio. I gave him the mean sloppy top in high school for a Marmot, he's been a ride or die ever since. LMAO! We remain cool, flirt here and there over the IG but not serious or physical. Well I was meeting up with him cause his dough was low and he was selling his Gucci watch. A $3,000 6 kt diamond, digital, water resistant, with white scratch resistant rubber strap for 2 bands, in the original box, receipt included, for 15 hundred if I throw some top in it, he joked but was dead ass. I didn't find his joke funny. He was questioning me and shit like he was my man or something. FOH! Niccas be sensitive! Worrying about the next nicca dick, worry about yourself! He blow the thought of me sucking on his dick! I paid the 2 bands and breezed on his corny ass. I tell

Tuesday, July 11th

y'all the watch is for the Harlem's chicken king but for Julio my mouth was shut. I call him the Harlem chicken king cause he owns 20 chicken spots in Harlem. Today is his birthday! Yes I drop 2 bands on him. He has done more for me than any nicca has even thought about doing for me. Ock has sponsored a 4 door 2008 Honda Civic SI for my 16th birthday after I finally passed the road test for my licenses. It took me 4 times to passing but I did it! And I was that bitch in high school whipping it! 85% of my classmate would never even rent a car much less own one in their life time. Teachers were even hating most of them were riding public transportation! LOL! You know niccas was hating cause I was the shit!!! I'm young and getting it! My car had been keyed a million time and the sad part is it could've been a student or even a teacher. Gabe busted out the windows twice on his jealous bully and got it fixed both times on his defender of our love bullshit. My car was a trap house on wheels, LOL. Niggas bag and smoked, and fucked and sucked all on the back seats, LOL! I really loved that car but after 18 months I totaled it, drinking and driving. Nobody was hurt but the thought of someone death on my hands has kept me from behind the wheel for the last 3 years. I appreciated Ock for the car but I loved him for the jelly that streamed out of bitches and niccas pores when their ears heard me pull up! LOL! one of Ock's cousins owned a car dealership I could've gotten another car but I dðjust was off driving for now. As my high school graduation present he gave my brownstone in BK, he owned the property, the tenants had moved out. I didn't just get to live in the brownstone my name was on the deed. Now this wasn't just no little ole brownstone, no no! My brownstone sits on the corner in Bay Ridge. On the street was a right side entrances to a studio apartment. I could rent it out but I didn't want to be neighboring with a total strange and I couldn't find nobody close enough to trust. Money has cost many relationships, so the studio apartment is currently empty. I last used the space to fuck Monty. LML! There are 12 outdoor stairs up from the street level, above the studio apartment, is my front door. My front door sits in the middle of 2 windows on each side. The 2 story, 3 bedroom, 2 full bathroom and a kitchen lined with all modern technology. I'm from the jets where there are no buttons on the stove there are knobs. There is no glass stove top, there are pilot lights, that I have lit with a burning brown paper bag. LOL! Upon entering the front door is a door less vestibule. On the left side and right side walls of the vestibule there are coat hooks, I leave my heels here, don't want to scratch up my hard wood floors. When I moved in here it was just an open space with no wall separating the 1st floor into sections. I had to make it a home with furniture. Straight ahead about 5 steps from the vestibule is the entrance to the marble countertop kitchen on the right side wall and 12 more steps are the stairs to the 2nd floor. Between the vestibule and the kitchen entrance I have a little glass table up against the wall, where I usually throw my keys, above the table is a huge mirror, this is where I get my last look before I walk out the door. To the left of the stairs to the 2nd floor is the "living room." The front wall in the living room is 100 feet of bare brick. I brought an electric fire place to put in front of the brick wall, it fits perfectly, it ass like the fire place was built in to the wall. Over the fire place is a mounted 80 inch TV, there was 2a nice gap in between the fireplace and the TV, I was able to have 3 shelves and the bare brick still be visible. A shelf for each electronic, the cable box, the blue ray player and the surround sound slash radio system. Gabe put up the shelves. To fill in the 10 feet of brick wall on both sides of the TV, there are 4 feet tall speakers and 6 feet lamps. See, to everyone that had viewed the property saw the bare brick wall as a negative feature but I had accentuated the elements into a positive light. The beauty of the bare brick exposed and highlighted. The TV and the surround sound slash radio system was all purchase on a discount from another one of Ock's cousins that owned an electronic store. The fire place and furniture were also purchased on a discount from another one of Ock's cousins. I set up the living room according to the length of the brick wall. On the right wall of the living room there are 2 windows. These windows are on the left side of the door if looking from outside. In front of the windows is a cappuccino colored chaise with wooden legs. The wooden legs on the chaise matched the wooden floors, to the lines, if some said they were cut from a different tree I would call them a lair to their face. On the left side is another cappuccino colored chaise and in front of fireplace on the floor I had a brick red rug with a wooden circle coffee table standing on it. The coffee table is in front of the paisley printed love seat. The loveseat had plenty of earth tones but the brick red and wooden brown were the boldest. I had paisley matching curtains in the windows behind the chaise. Behind the loveseat is my home made walk path and my mini bar up again the stair case wall. To the left of the bar is the downstairs bathroom, no bathtub just shower with a glass door. Pass the chaise on the left side is the "dining room." I have a high round table that seats 4 in front of the window on the fireplace wall. I have a thing for zebra stripes so the seat of chairs, the square floor rug and curtain were all zebra stripe. Upstairs there was 3 bedrooms when I moved in. I asked another one of Ock's cousin that works in construction to build me a window seat and break down a wall to make one bed room out of 2 bed rooms and he did a hellva job. LOL! He took out a door and built a wall, no one would even know my rooms was once 2 rooms. In front of the stairs on the 2nd floor is a window and to the right are stairs leading to the roof top. There was 3 bedrooms, one over the kitchen, one over the living room and one over the dining room. The room over the dining room I converted into a walking closet. The door to the closet is on the left wall. Walk down the hallway to my room door. My room was shaped like a U after I took out the wall. The entrance is in the middle of the hoop of the U. The left side of my room is over the kitchen. The left side has the bathroom right behind the inward opening door to my room. Bathroom is so big I have a vanity table with chair set inside. So I picked the left side to put my queen size bed with a huge gold crown as a head broad in the center of the room, up against the left wall, my bed was facing the inside of the U. on both side of my bed are sets of double windows. TV and entertainment center straight across from the bed. The best part of my room is the foot wide pink and red stripes on the walls. Me and Gabe painted the walls but it looked like it was done by professionals. My room is plain, bed, end tables, lamps, and a dresser. My bedroom is for fucking or sleeping thats it. LOL! On the right side of the U, over the living room had the beautiful brick wall. I created an office area, with a desk and computer. To the left is my lovely window seat. I bought huge round doggy bed to give the window seat cushioning, it fits perfectly. I had room for something else in this

room but what? I haven't figured it out yet.
Now my favorite part of the house, is the
rooftop. It has a huge wooden picket fence with
spikes pointing to the sky to keep the city's
pigeons from nesting and shitting on my shit.
The picket fence roof was covering a plush pink
L shape sofa. Ock's cousin had to use a mini
crane to get the couch on the rooftop. I bought
a red couch just to take the back and seat
pillow just to have as throw around seats on the
roof top. I also had some bean bags and a mini
bar. I loved the roof top a lot of hot summer
nights I have sleep out here. Yes I have fuck
out here too. I hear you talking smack but it's
not the same as with Trenton. We were fucking
at street level the roof top is higher up, FYI!
So what you think? Do Ock deserve a little
Gucci watch that cost 2 bands? Ock don't ask
for much just some pussy and top on his
birthday and Valentine's Day. one time has he
ever called me outside of these 2 dates, and
I've been fucking with Ock for over 5 years
now. I know I was making his day by pulling up
to his job with the watch and balloons it was
written all over his face. Ock wasn't easy on the
eyes. He had skinny arms and legs with a big pop
round beer belly. I don't know if it was the belly

in his way but his dick was a stout 5 by 5. I can't give a rating on his dick cause I have never felt it. I have squeeze my pussy lips tight and still nothing. When we fuck his big belly bumps into my ass and his sweat smelled like the parsley and mint in Tabbouleh salad. Tabbouleh salad is Ock's favorite mid-eastern dish. His underarms goes from 0 to 100 real quick. LML! And under his belly smells like spoiled cottage cheese. While I'm sucking his uncircumcised dick that smell like old hot dog water, his cottage cheese belly be rubbing the top of my weave. The combination of all the rotten food always fucked with my stomach. I be feeling nauseous for 2 hours afterward. He was so grateful for the watch. He only desired me to give him head today. We went to his back office and my lips did all the talking. My lips had him crying creamy tears. It felt so good to Ock that he greased my hand with a 500 dollars, cause my weave was finished. Today he feel the need to be playing, pulling and stinking it up my hair. I hit Gucci, my hair stylist, up immediately. My next stop was the hood. I had to check up on Louie grease monkey ass. LOL. After seeing Louie I ran into Cali. Cali is part of the B.A.D bitch team we ran hard with each other one summer. Someway somehow, we just keep losing contact. Cali lived life like I did from dollar to dick. Me and Cali crashed Earl's crib. I needed to smoke to settle my stomach after Ock. It was just a lot, that belly, little uncircumcised dick, and he stink! Brah!! Pick a struggle! LMAO! We chilled smoked and laugh at Earl and his busted friends until it was time for Cali to go to work. She worked at a strip club in Queens. She gave me her updated phone number. I couldn't wait to get home to tell Naturel I ran in Cali. It was 10 at night and I was bored. I didn't work tonight and didn't have a nothing lined up. So I'm home lonely posting selfie. LMAO! Then April hit me up. You remember April, the ATL girl from the Emery tour. She was in my city and wanted me to come out and play. She had hooked up with a party promoter. She caught the promoter's eye while working Emery's tour. She was hosting a new artist listening party in Manhattan. She promised free entry, unlimited alcohol and the hope of getting some dick I was coming up on my 78th hour since being fucked properly by Earl and my pussy was furious with me. Yeah, yeah I fucked Chipy last night but that was more of a learn experience than a sex-perience.

LMAO!! I dolled up right quick, called the call service and was on my way in one hour. It was a dim lighted club, closed to public, exclusive event. I greeted April she set me up in a corner and went back to work she came back every 10 minutes with a shot of liquor in her hand to check up on me. I was peeping who was on deck and available. My pussy was determined to get some dick tonight. My concentration was broken by the flash of a camera's light. The hired photographer was admiring my image. My pussy was favorable to his fresh haircut. The hairline with precise razor sharp lines. My eyes could smell the barbicde on him. My pussy been crying for Bengee. But now it was throwing a tantrum thanks to the photographer's hair line caused my pussy remising over Bengee. It was something about a fresh haircut that made my pussy bleed white. I didn't want to go through the minor conversation to get to the major fucking. So I asked straight up. He valued honesty and my honesty made the value in his dick rise. There were blind spots in the club we found one. I lift my dress up to my waist and sat on his dick, with my back facing him. I rolled my hip to feed my pussy all he had to offer. As the pleasure level increase so did the rhythm of my hips. I hammered the dick with my pussy. He was heaving his hips up in the air. I bounce harder. I was grateful the music was so loud nobody could hear my ass cheek and pussy clapping on and off the dick. I was pulverizing that dick until the guts shot out into the condom. I hopped up off the slow shrinking dick and breezed from the scene of the sex-perience. LML! I left him pants open, dick out and a disoriented expression on his face looking like a rape victim. LMAO! I hug April good night and hopped in my awaiting car. The whole ride home I was ode thinking about Bengee. The photographer nursed my pussy, it wasn't happy but was quiet. My mind harbored thoughts of Bengee swimming in my head. I indulged in the thoughts while taking a nice bath. I lit the scented candles around my tub and soaking in Bengee memories. TTYL!

Today is a busy day for me. I have a lot of run-a-rounds before work. 1st I posted my WCW, which is Gucci, my hair stylist, sistah and idol. A lot of dancer's super hero is Anna Nichole Smith, Black china or Amber colored rose but Gucci is my hero. Gucci can cook, give 2 kids a bath, braid hair, sell cloths she boosted, roll a blunt, talk on the phone, fuck a nicca, jerk a dick or flip a female's clit, give head to two nicca, and still had room to spit all at the same time while maintaining two steady pay checks from stripping at a club and selling drugs. Now tell me thats not a B.A.D bitch! Gucci was fucking with this nicca she had met at the club that had bands on bands. He died on top of her literally. He had a spontaneous heart attack. Now that's what you call killer pussy. LMAO! JK! He had left Gucci all his money in his will. The woman he lived with for 10 years and moms of his 3 kids with wasn't even listed in the will but the kids were. The wife try to take Gucci to court for a piece of the bread but was unsuccessful. LML! Gucci pussy worth to him was in print. In Gucci words "A pussy print" speak louder than words. LOL! I also took the time to hit Sundae up about her video shoot! LOL! Me and April joked about her last night.

Wednesday, July 12ᵗʰ

No reply back, yet! Bengee hit me up wanting to have lunch. It was like he could hear my pussy crying out for him. I definitely wanted to see him but I was nervous about it. After Jah little fucking show Monday morning at Midnights. I couldn't wait til I get to work tonight to black on his ass. Bragging about pussy he didn't even get! LMAO! I was nervous that Jah's words had changed Bengee's view of me. Usually I don't give a fuck what people has to say about me but with Bengee, his opinion mattered. Ask me why? And I'll tell you I don't know why? It just did. We were having lunch at the olive garden on forty deuce. We banquet on words of our past. I felt free with my words it was a similar feeling of talking to one of the gurls minus the judgmental stares. The more he talked the more I wanted to consume his babies, suck them right from his longings. His intelligence mixed with his articulation was immaculate. Mind you he hadn't finish high school. He obtained his GED in prison. His heart made a wrong decision and landed him in jail. I ingested his scent, the softness of the inside of his hand, the piercing of his words and knife cutting hairline with the money Mitch part. He was a nickel and dime hustler but now he was paid in full through his scaffolding job. I wanted him to put his balls on my chin so I could get the sex ball rolling. All he had to do was give the eye and I'll could handle the rest but my wants wouldn't leap from my mouth like the desire was verbalizing down my tight. Me and Bengee parted with a long partake in a hug. My pussy was crying with jealousy from the hug, it felt left out, it needed to be hugged too. LML! As I was walking away from Bengee his image transported to memory. My attention was caught by a text from Scott the basketball/football coach. Coach Scott is a white man in love with the coco! Aye! Bnut try to keep it on the low low! LMAO! He loved chocolate women but married vanilla. Once in a while he gets a craving for some chocolate that's when my phone start whistle blowing. He was also old news but my pussy had a new thirst for Bengee. I had to hydrate, and quickly, Coach Scott will have to do. So I answered Coach Scott's text. I agreed to meet up with him at his office, which is a gym, in Harlem. When I got there he was showering in the team showers. I stood and watch the soapy water trickle down his pigskin colored dick and balls. The rest of his body was pink as a pig but his genitals was naturally tanned. In the past I've toyed with him and called him cookie and cream. His complexion was cream colored but his dick and style was chocolate all the way. He must of fumbled the ball at home and been forced to slumber at work. LMAO! If I was a man it would be no way in hell a woman would put me out of the home I pay the bills for. FOH! Anyway I stood in the door arch facing the row of showers heads, 5 on the left wall and 5 on the right wall. Scottie was standing up under the 3rd shower head on the right wall. I was wet from the view of Scottie's pale skin redden up from the drapes of steamy water bumps flowing from the shower head. I strip out of my clothes and joined Scottie. I had a hair appointment next Monday so I didn't mind getting my weave wet and rocking it curly for few days. He must have felt me pulling up on him cause he turned around. His hands and hard helmet player embraced me and my pussy with sexual ambition. I wrapped my arms around his neck. He pinned my back up against the wet shower wall while his face nuzzled in my neck inhaling my coco scent. He tossed his pigskin in my pussy. The fog that surrounded us could have been the stream from the water, the heat of the moment or the smoke from how fast Scottie's player was running in my pussy. With my thighs in his hand he kicked off with deep launches of the pigskin. I applauded his hits to my marked g-spots. The water cascade down our wet bodies. I sopped up the sexual lust of the touching and the sight of our complexions alongside each other. His helmet player blitz through the storm of creamy rain pouring down on his head. He released my legs and turned me around. I bent over, outstretched my right legs, and held on to ankles with my hand. It looked like I was doing a ballerina stretch. He entered my pussy nice and slow. He rested his hand on my ass cheeks. He tackled this pussy with straight hits. My pussy shout the squishy squashy sound of ecstasy. He bombard my pussy walls with an excursion to the field goal. He squeezed my ass cheeks open and my pussy walls closed in on his player. The player ran inside and out collecting yardage in this pussy. My ass cheeks sprung back and forth in the air off his stomach franticly. His moans was soft but he came hard. He was half turned on by my tight pussy's wall and the other half was my honey dipped chocolate flavored skin. I wringed out my hair and was prepared to leave almost forgetting why I came here in the 1st place. I wanted to use his job's rooftop basketball court for Ivory's birthday party. The building had an elevator, a plus with her wheelchair situation. He agreed but shorted me 2 hundred dollars. He generous with the dick but stingy with the money. I really need a nap before going to work and swinging from another pole. LMAO! I just took my shower now, I'll BRB!

Last night my car service hit me with a curb, it was a new driver Tau. Tau means lion in Sotho an African dialect. A sexy tall African, with a heavy accent dressed up in up to date American clothes. Okay I see you! It was easy to convince him a professional dick suck was better than money with my technique of massaging words to make it feel good. LMAO! I sucked his dick with pleasure. He had a foreign size dick. I enjoy slurping on his long solid foreign chocolate stick. Once he came I had to go but reserved time so my pussy could feed on the exquisite foreign chocolate too. As soon as I walked through the door Jah was all in my face with apologizes! FOH! Why was he even talking to me? I don't with fuck you, you stupid ass bitch nicca. Turned out on pussy he didn't even get. LMAO! I laughed in his healing black eye. He had stepped way out of line and Bengee knocked his bitch ass in back in to position. I had nothing to say to Jah. Giving him my words was a donating to much of my time. Jah is a buffoon that makes me laugh on sight. I ain't even mad at him for being himself, a fucking clown. Wednesday nights are slow but in the summertime you can see timber weeds roll through there. It was a $600 and some change type of night and that include stage tips and lap dance tips. And I had to work my twerk and clap my ass twice ass hard to get that chump change. But the night picked right on up when Tau scooped me. He already knew where I lived so my brown stone was the best option. I took him to the studio apartment. I hopped up on the kitchen marble countertop and pulled him between my legs. My pussy drool from the taste of the foreign chocolate that was tasted by my mouth. My hand was gravitated to the exotic chocolate. I wrapped the chocolate in the gold package latex and there was still uncovered chocolate skin. I eased my slobbering pussy on to the chocolate. I wrapped my legs around his back and crossed my feet. My legs control the sway of the foreign beat. Once my pussy was familiar with the flow of the foreign melody I raised my legs to his shoulders. His eyes brightened over my flexibility of my legs and pussy walls. He was clobbering this pussy with that foreign size dick. My pussy's lips eat up the foreign chocolate pass the wrapper. The foreign tune had a hardcore bass line that was recorded into my pussy and vibrated through my body. The 4 heavy strokes from oversea caused him to overflow in the wrapper. He try to linger around but my pussy was full and I was catching the itis. LOL! He questioning why there was no furniture besides a bed. I explained it away as financial struggles. LMAO! He was eager to help. I gladly took his money, the little 400 dollars and was thankfully for it but I was more grateful for the foreign chocolate. The chocolate was more valuable than the little chump change. The foreign chocolate was sex-tra extra, Yummy! LOL! I went upstairs to my real home and showered, LOL, and slept like a baby! I woke up in a good mood this morning, pussy was silent. LOL Tau laid the smack down on this pussy, for real! I had breakfast on the rooftop. When I was on my way to kitchen to put the dirty dishes in the sink, I passed my moms picture from when she was 19 years old. I pass this picture all the time but today it stood out, so I posted it to IG for TBT. It's a head shot of my moms. You can read the innocents in her eyes. Bright with rainbows of love, birds chirping C Breezy in her ear. Gia is a mirror of my moms at 19, not only in age and in verbatim facial features but in life status. My moms was at the high of her gymnastic career. Beautiful black woman, Olympic gold medalist on every magazine cover in the world.

Thursday, July 13th

My grandmother had invested her whole life to my mom's career. She was so proud of my moms the day she know was coming had finally arrived. The blood, sweat and tears was being reward and it was 10 times more valuable than the medals them self. So imagine the hurt when my mother decided to throw her career away for puppy love with my father, her assistant Trainer. An older man not married but was in a few situations with other women. You know them teams travel the world. SMFH! My father was all good with fucking fresh 19 yrs old pussy but when my moms announced that she was pregnant and was putting her career on hold shit changed real quick. Them rainbows turned into clouds of regret and the birds was sing a different tune in Keyshia Cole's voice. My father thugged it out for 14 yrs. They both lived under the same roof when my father wasn't skipping around the world with team but the love that makes walls into a home just wasn't there. They lived separate lives both sleeping around. Don't mistake me we lived like any other family. With broad games, TV time, and one on one conversations. I wasn't deprived of a childhood. I plenty of great memories of us ice skating, Easter egg hunting, and fun times at the beach. The connection between my parents always felt off. I 'm not saying they didn't share affection with each other cause I've seen them kiss, even caught them fucking a few times. Ewe! I also witnessed each of them sneak to fuck other people. Neither one of them wanted to be there but was there for us, Goldie, myself and Gia. My moms was a housewife while my father continued Training the team. When my father left my grandfather, from my father side would step in. He is an extra sweet old man. There wasn't nothing he wouldn't do for me or Goldie. He was me and Goldie's father for real when my father jump ship overseas with Gia. He keep the peace between me and Goldie. We just couldn't get along. But when granddad die so did the peace between me and Goldie. I never said it before but I wanted to go to Russia, even though I know the circumstances I still had a little hate toward my father for just bouncing. My thoughts was interrupted by a knock at my door. I went to the kitchen and grabbed my pepper stray just in case it was Monty's punk ass. Its wasn't Monty's bitch ass it was 2 homicide DTs, a short chocolate man named Hasle with the sexiest dark chocolate lips,

Thursday, July 13th

yummy and a bitch named Pikins with a stink attitude. "Would you like to put some clothes on?" is what she said. Hello this is my fucking house! How you going to come to my shit uninvited and tell me what the fuck to wear? Police just be over stepping the line. If I want to parade around my house in a g-string with no top that's my fucking BI, right? I grab my zebra printed robe maybe I was intimidating her with all this sexiness, LMAO!! They pulled out Monty's picture and asked me did I know him? My 1st thought was damn Tank I wanted you scare the nicca not fucking kill him. Shit!! But the DTs calmed my nerves and gave me the only drop on Monty. Monty bitch ass was obsessed with his ex. She broke up with him and stabbed her to death and killed his own 2 kids. All cause he saw her with her new nicca WOOOOOW! He broke into to her apartment and waiting for her to come home. He stabbed her 97 times and slit the throats of his son and daughter. Can you fucking believed that I fucked a fucking serial killer? They arrested him trying to break into my house a few days ago. I sat there with my fucking mouth open in disbelief. I couldn't believe my pussy almost got me killed. Here I'm think Monty bitch ass was harmless when the muther fucker was a wolf in sheep clothing. Speaking highly of his wife and kids like they were living. WOW! I couldn't wait to tell the gurls about Monty bitch ass over Glammaris cocktales. LOL! We meet up at Black's condo on 97th street on west end ave. Black's crib is crack with the floor to ceiling windows. I've been to Black's apartment plenty of time but I'm usually helping Natural move her shit out. This time is one of the few times it was pleasure and not pain. When I got there everybody was here. Cali, Gucci, Kourtney and of Naturel. They were waiting on me to mix my signature drink. It makes me feel nice but lit. I wouldn't give the recipe no matter how much they beg but I give to you, it's :

¼ cup of Svedka vodka
one/3 cup of Alize red passion
½ bright and early orange drink

Pour it over crushed ice and you will have the Glammaris sex-perience. LOL! We get together and share cocktails over cocktales. Kourtney broke the ice with her tale of the cock she's fucking. Here's the put on about Kourtney, she's the good school girl. She's been with her man since high school. They finally moved into together but no kids. They both want to finish college, get good jobs before cooking a bun. Her cocktale was he don't help out around the house or go to the store. All relationships are based off of the dick or the whips of the pussy. Let me explain, a nicca with a big dick ain't cleaning or going to the store cause he put in all work in the bedroom. Now a nicca that can't fuck is cleaning, cooking, store runs and feet rub downs. LMAO! Now if you whipping that pussy and mouth right you can get any nicca to do anything. LOL!!! Cali was next up on the mic. She crying over a nicca she claiming and he claims to be claiming her but ain't no proof of that. She been fucking the nicca for 5 yrs and never been to his house, never met his family or friends and the last slap in the face is no outdoor appearance with her on his arm. C'mon!! Ray Charles can see through that with Stevie Wonder's glasses. But like I say a nicca that lay down dreams in the bedroom will make a believer out of of a bitch in a heartbeat. LOL! It was my turn cause Gucci wasn't going to air her dirty sex-perience cause like most woman she is afraid of the labels that come with being a woman in tuned with your sexuality. It's crazy a man can get praise for smashing mad chick but a chick is a thot for doing the same thing. I just love fucking, so I fuck a lot LOL! Thot has a different meaning in Glammaris's world

T- things

H- happen

O- out

T- there

If a nicca get my pussy jumping hard enough I'm going to want to fuck. I shouldn't have to wear a label for that! Right? I breezed on the gurls didn't want to hear Naturel story I lived it, LOL! Plus I had to get ready to slide down some poles, some metal some flesh! LOL! BRB

Friday, July 14th

Last night was a slow night. Thank god for LMS boos. I walked out of the club with 500 funk ass dollars and Nicolas ass was my driver. I was so tight I went home and went straight to bed. NOT A GOOD NIGHT!! But this morning I woke to a good morning beautiful text from Bengee. I was instantly wet for the day. LML! He asked if I would go with him doll shopping for his 9 year old daughter. We settled on meeting at F.A.O Swartz at 3 ish. I showered and got dressed. I had to stop in the hood to buy the bottles for Earl's fight party tomorrow night. He bought some fight off of pay-per-veiew and invited a bunch of niccas. They had bet chart going on and everything. Earl's birthday is in December he is not 21 yet. He had the money he just needed my ID. I didn't mind doing little favors for Earl we are friends. Plus I had to stop by grease monkey Louie ass for my coins and checkup Mr. Buster. I will be attending Earl's party. You know niccas get drink and go from mildly ignorant to straight up retarded, real quick. I was sure to get a drink, a good laugh, and might see a live fight. Nicca go crazy over money. My pussy and stomach had the tizzies for the thought of seeing Bengee. I had to hurry up and fuck him so I could forget about him. This constant ache to want to be near him can't be healthy. My pussy has an endless slobbering for his dick, I wanted so bad I could almost taste him even in my thoughts. Yeah I got to fuck him out of my system. When I reach the meeting spot. I stood on the corner still as a broad with anticipation as my stomach does cartwheels. He crept up behind me and covered my eyes. I'm body so thirsty for his sexual touch that I fell back into him just to brush by the bulge that called my name. We joked around in the store with a variety of toys. I giggled at his jokes as my pussy cackled with creamy tears of anxiousness. His loveable scent caused the whimpering between my legs. We picked up a few Barbie's and when it was time to part ways I went in for the hug and kiss on the cheek but he moved his face and my lips landed on his lips. I turned white and sheepish. I breezed on him. OMG! I can't believe he kissed me and I ran. I didn't foresee him doing that I just wasn't prepared for a kiss from Bengee. Hell yeah I want to fuck his brains out, drink his babies and make him a sandwich right after but I guess in my mind I was the one to make the 1st move. I beating my own ass for that bozo move. My pussy is really cussing me out. Tyree little young

Friday, July 14th

ass text me he got a free crib his moms ain't home. Tyree is the young tender I meet while I was at Mickey d's with Gia, remember? I hailed a cab on the street. yes I was ducking Tau. I don't want nobody else to beat this pussy up but Bengee. I was going to put it down on Tyree little young ass. LOL! He was just practice. Tyree was no match for this pussy. I breastfeed on his above average size dick. I sucked on it crazily. No steady sequence just free styling on the mic. I lick the head during breaks from the inside of my mouth, the tears flowed freely. I pushed him back on his young twin size mattress. I climb on top off him. He whined while I winded this pussy on his young dick. He sex-perienced 3 series of large amounts of wailing and heavily whining bursting from his every point in his body. It was illogical the amount and the number of times his eye cried creamy tears. After I got dress I looked back at his younger tender ass sucking his thump fast asleep his eye all cried out. LMAO!!! I sprung him around with my pussy like a mother bounce her kid on her knee. He is 18 but in sex-perience a he is a toddler. He is a young tender bone running through quantity of young pussy humping like a mad rabbit. He never had a slow grind from quality pussy. He never been in a slobbering throbbing thirsty beast before. My superiority worn me out I had to put my back into, just to show the youngun how to shot. LOL! Now he know how things goes on the flipside. He use to sparring with them young bitches but today he got knocked out LOL. I had to crudité his little ass as an appetizer now I'm ready for the main course Bengee sexy ass. I'm going to get that dick, watch me! I need a little shut eye before work. I'm legs was tried and my mind was too from the running thoughts of Bengee. I am just exasperated. TTYL.

Saturday, July 15th

Last at the club them bitches keep it lit. Sugar claims her gold bracelet was missing and Pepsi picked it up. Now she got Black popping people locks on their locker looking for the bracelet. Sugar bumped Pepsi with her shoulder and all hell broke loose. Cinnamon hooked off on Cherri just cause Pepsi was her peeps. I told y'all this shit is like high school, bitches is clicked up. It's just dumb shit. Hair pulling, tities popping out, and all for nothing. Bitches be fronting like they don't need the bread but be early birds to work every shift. FOH! But yet fighting at work. Yes I went back to my car service and Tau was the driver. It was 90 outside and in the car it was a sweltering 100 degrees with sexual tension. My pussy was having an anxiety attack foaming and leaking for some of Tau's outlandish foreign chocolate. But I composed my pussy with the tranquilizing thought of Bengee. But I did taunt my thirst with a taste of the exotic chocolate with rich creamy insides. I looked like a little kid that just finished eating an ice cream cone. I had a ring of cream around my mouth falling slowly down onto my lips. My fingertip's dribbling of cream from my hand attraction to the smooth texture of the chocolate. After I topped him off he dropped me off at home. I showered. But I was still lit off the molly I popped earlier. I couldn't go out cause I didn't trust my pussy. So I went to the roof top and had a few drinks. I passed out up there I woke up in the am it like 9 am. I went to my bed to sleep til one. When I was fully up I realized I was drunk texting Bengee at like 4 in the morning. OMG! The thirst be so real! LMAO!!! Thank God I didn't text anything too crazy. But I did promise him lunch, that I was to bring to his job site. I ran around like a chicken with my head cut off. I couldn't find nothing. It was crazy! But it always happen like that! I see something every day for a week as soon as I decide I want to wear it, I can't find it! That ever happen to you? I finally got out of the fuckin house and into the car service Nicholas was the fucking driver. Where the fuck is Mohammed or even Tau. Mohamed was having back surgery and Tau was off. Bengee was working on 73rd and 5th ave today. His site change daily. I was so amp to smell his scent and stare in to his eyes dreaming of swallowing his seeds that I complete forgot about the awkward pretend kiss. Standing face to face with had the tizzies going crazy in my stomach and pussy. The palm of my hands was sweating.

Saturday, July 15th

I was leaking from everywhere. I handed him the sandwich in the brown bag and a bottled Welsh's grape soda. We walked through Central Park. It was a beautiful day. The sun shining bright but the air was cool not hot and humid. Talking to each other was therapeutic for both of us. To speak my mind freely without the critical eyes looking down on me or the hypocritical advice from lips. The mist of the awkward kiss hung over us like a cloud. I started to bring it up but was stopped by his tongue slithering around in my mouth. His saliva was like holy water blessing me with his lustful desires. He pulled me close and wrapped his arms above my ass. I wrapped my arms around his neck and squeezed just to make sure I wasn't dreaming. I could feel the sexual heat arise in his pants. Thru drooling lips my pussy expressed the craving of throwing him on the ground and sucking his crop dry of seeds. He pulled back from my grip it was time for him to go back to work. my pussy bawled at the sight of him walking away. From Central park I took a cab to my brownstone I had about 4 hours before Earl's fight party. OMG I was in Bengee's arms with his tongue down my throat!!!!! I can't wait to fuck the shit out of

Saturday, July 15th

him!!! I had to sleep off the thirst, my pussy's steadily crying had given me a headache. I woke up rejuvenated and my pussy's thoughts refreshed. Don't get me wrong my pussy craved Bengee but wasn't crying about. It was 9 pm I lounged around my brownstone before I popped a molly, got dressed and headed to Earl's crib. Nicholas dropped me off in the hood. I stopped by my moms to check up on the kids and swung by Mr. Busters too. Everybody were where they suppose to have been. Earl's apartment had wall to wall painted with hood niccas. About 50 niccas and 10 hood chicks all turned to watch me enter. 120 eyes balling me my eyes stared back. My eye spy a bunch of clown ass niccas, sharing ass niccas. Dick swing in another nicca pair of trues but you lying like they belong to you. Under arms and feet ringing in another nicca's shirt and sneakers but you scream you the man. Rocking a cubin link once a week cause it belong to your man. Pretending to be someone your not, rocking another nicca's style and intend to return it back. Get your bread off credit card scams walking around with a money knot allusion, $300 broken down to one hundred dollar bill, 2 fifty dollar bills 5 twenty dollar bills and a 100 singles. Bragging, claiming you moving weight but its grams that you split with your man. Lying on you dick, when it's only a 4 by 4 stick when its stuff. Clown ass niccas staring at my ass but don't have the cash or in the right class to get in this ass. And the hood chick no better staring at me like I came to steal their shine cause they are working the room. Fake model chicks, "For bookings" in their IG bio, but they only spread their legs for pigeon size bread. Fronting like your brand is up but got fake Gucci on shoulder, waist and eyes. Where your bread at? Fucking niccas in crib while your kids is home for coins but demand respect from your kids. Twerk vids on the IG, living 4 to bed but chase dick is all you see ahead. Hood chicks and nicca watched my every move, there eye shot dart of pure hate, I laugh cause their dart never touched my skin, HAHA!!!! Earl wanted to brag about our friends by making noise over my seat. Making niccas clear my path. He actually made a nicca get up so I could sit down. He hopped around me making sure I was comfortable, smoking and sipping. Earl's fight party delivered everything expected. A unlimited supply of liquor. A few good chuckles. You know in a group of niccas there's going to be some shots fired. Shot are jokes but they really hurt. Aye yo! The nicca said "his dick is a dead muscle cause it gets no excise, pause" LMAOOOO! Flamed him. Of course a nicca drink too much and be on that go dumb shit start fighting over blunts, shots turn into bullets, you know the regular hood shit. LML! So tonight's fight off the screen was 2 niccas, usally its 2 hood chicks. one nicca was fucking the other nicca moms, while he was away at college. So the college nicca came home for the summer and you know niccas put him on ASAP and then shit got rocky. LMAO! So the college nicca was extra tight cause the nicca fucking his moms was keeping up with him, and never said a word about him piping his moms, SMFH! So they finally bumped heads at Earl's fight party and the college nicca popped that bottle on the bitch ass nicca and the fight begun. Earl and his friends broke up the fight and throw them the fuck out. I sat and smoked and sipped comfortably, chuckling the whole time. While all this is going on this bird ass nicca Peanut is chipping in my ear. Peanut is the kid that got picked on as a child, and while he was growing up and got his money up, now he think his that nicca. Brah!! GTFOH! You was nobody then and you are invisible now. He started complimenting

Saturday, July 15th

me from my shoes to my eye lashes, just being ode annoying. Brah! Are you serious? Finally his words caught my attention. He said verbatim "I got a band and a half for you but I gotta recorded it! HAHA you aint gonna zoe me like you did Jah stupid ass HAHA!" and the remaining niccas chimed in with their outburst of laughter. My eyes looked straight at Earl's ugly ass! I only told his ugly ass that I zoed Jah's clown ass and written down in this book. And even on 5 mollys I know these white pages don't talk. Earl I have one question WHY? I know them big lip have a hard time holding food but words too? We have been friends since 5th grade and you shit on my like that? WOW? I was so tight all eyes was on me and my slanted eyes was throwing daggers at Earl's bitch ass. Then Earl's brother, Elton, walked thru the door and all the attention was thrown to him. Earl trying to walk over to explain but I had made a deal with Peanut to taste my pussy for 7 hundred in Earl's bathroom. Fuck Earl he didn't want to dance with me, he's the sensitive one. I'll leave holes all through his heart with my heels. Earl standing outside the bathroom door with the Stevie J lips. Nicca please ain't nobody scared of your ugly ass twisting up your face.

Saturday, July 15th

He questioning me did I fuck in his bathroom? I'm keeping my fucking mouth shut! I know he was outside the door listening like a creep. Peanut's tongue game was about a 6 but I moaned like it was a 20. LMAOOO. I only dragged my tongue a crossed the head and a few jerks and the nicca nutted, too easy. I wouldn't even say I gave him head I played with his dick. LML! A bunch of fucking clowns! On my way out the door Earl's brother Elton offered me a ride. I was going to decline but I saw Earl's eyes turn red with envy and his hand balled with anger, so I accepted the ride. Elton is the complete opposite of Earl. Elton is 24 or 25 yrs old. He's tall like Earl but his face is pretty. Perfect eyebrows, button nose, and thin lips. But Elton was off limits for 2 reasons. He's Earl's brother for number one and 2nd he is Ivory's 1st baby father, not the one that shot her in the back. But he was one pretty nicca. I only took the ride to fuck with Earl. I couldn't believe him. The whole ride Elton gloated about his daughter that he shared with Ivory. I been half listening and writing, LOL! Well I'm here at the club. BRB!!!

Sunday, July 16th

Saturday night at the club was sex-tra extra lit. LMAO!!!! I had popped 2 mollys I was so mad at Earl. How could he open his fucking ugly mouth? I tell you hoes just ain't loyal! I was kinda nervous coming into work. All night I was waiting for Jah to confront me but it never happened. I was so lit of the alcohol, molly and the music that I share the stage with Cherri. I don't be dancing with bitches cause you got to slit the tip and last night my LMS boos were squad deep. We made a band off one song. Ass and tities were on fleek!!! I hated having to split the money. I'm not doing that again. Some nondescript nicca was my driver last night. Shit, I didn't mind paying cash for my ride to and from the club. My pussy was all cried out waiting on Bengee's dick. I made the 1st move by texting him at like 6 in the morning. I was up on that triple H, high, hit and horny! I had to fuck Bengee right out of my system and get back to my life style of fucking these hoe niccas, getting this money and keeping my clothes on fleek. LMAO! Bengee was all my pussy cried about. He finally texted a invite to his house for bunch. I showered the smell of the club off my skin and tried to sleep last night of but it was hard with triple H and the molly floating through my body. My pussy was all worked up finally we was going to get some Bengee. I took my time with my hair, face and outfit. I walked out the door #flawlessonfleek! LMAO. I got there at 2 in the afternoon. I arrived to a well put together meal on his balcony. A glass table set for two. Sliced fruit, wine, homemade chicken and waffles. Trigger throwing musical sexual shots at my pussy, while my mouth thirsty to taste Bengee's skin. We chit chat about nothing over our food. I could no longer hold back my pussy once he filled my mouth with his tongue, again. The passion in his kiss was so strong, my knees were weak. His top lip pressed firm above my top lip and his fresh fruit flavored tongue filled my mouth. His right hand cupped the right side of my face and his left hand slide my weave out my eyes. It felt like he was reading my thoughts thru his fingertips. He spun me around to inhale the view of central park from the 32nd floor. With his arms crossed over my chest I brushed my ass up against his package. His lips planted wet kisses on my cheek as his teeth took playful bites down the back of my neck and on my shoulder. My pussy was hissing in his ear as my mouth heckled for taste of his babies. He excused himself and returned protected and ready. He forced his snake into the gates of my garden from behind. I gripped the rail on the balcony. The jingle of shoelace's metal hoop on his $\frac{3}{4}$ beef and broccoli colored tims was chiming with his body shifting. The clinking was driving me sexual senses insane my body screeched. He shhhed me by covering my mouth with his hand. His left hand squeezing my side. He swayed with the wind up, down, inside and out and the ringing of his boots sang along. The snake wondered deep inside my body, traveling way pass my pelvis bone. My legs shake from the steady clapping of his tights on my ass cheeks. He turned my body sideways and lift my right leg up onto the balcony rail. My hands gripped the left side of the rail as my garden closed in on the snake. I took my leg down from the rail. He quickly turned me around. He slide his tongue in my mouth again. He leaded me by the hand to his bedroom. When we entered the bedroom, he shut the windows and cut off his phone. Oh shit it was on! I was going to get his undivided attention. We locked lips again. As his tongue explore every corner of my mouth his hands discover parts of my skin. His hands touch every place I needed it the most. He kissed me down to the bed. My mouth watered to taste his snake. As I sat on the edge of the bed he feed the snake to my mouth with his right hand. I hungrily nourished on the snake like it was the last super. Savoring every lick. The snake threatened to spit. He pried the snake from the grasp of my lips. The snake spanked my lips for almost liquefy sensational pleasure. The beating excited the craving in my taste bubs even more and I sucked the head of the snake until a tear of joy fell from his eye. He climb on top of me and the snake found his way back in my tree less rain forest. The snake slither into spots I didn't know existed. I looked up at the mirror ceiling. The reflection of his evenly spread dark chocolate skin glistening and the curve in his spine like a serpent as his snake jigged at my emotions. My moans encourage the snake to hunt inside my body for more of uncontrollable creamy explosions. The snake rummage thru my cream and shouts, traveling deeper into my soul. My mouth and pussy hissed at the snake. My hands cuddle his dark caesar, with the money Mitch half-moon part as I embrace the snake with my creamy pussy hugs and plant kisses on his face. He flipped me over to my stomach. The snake wiggled back into my stomach. My cream run over the snake. He then inserted is index finger on his right hand into my rectum. I had never partaken in the anal game but I was so stimulated I throw my ass back on the snake and his finger. His index finger turn into two fingers then three fingers. My cream was gushing everywhere. He had awaken unknown pleasure. He replaced the three finger with the snake. He used his right hand to assist the snake and his left to keep me produce cream by fondling my pussy. The sluggish strokes turn to staunch blows of passion. He used both hands to part my ass cheeks so the snake could travel deeper in the forbidden muddy garden. I was biting the pillow and fingering my pussy for the ability to take the snake's journey. My finger could feel the snake's stomach scales through my pussy's wall the feeling elevated my orgasms. When I came my ears popped like when you ride the elevator to the last floor in the empire state building. After several discoveries of unchartered areas the snake jerks from injecting sweet venom into my soul. The snake had taken me on a tourism of multiple orgasmic adventures. I was mentally and physically drained. Y'all know I'm 1st to cum and 1st the leave. But I just couldn't move. I must've of dosed off cause when I open my eyes he was standing in front of me with shower bubbles on his shoulder and chest. He lift me up out of the bed and carried me to the master bathroom that was inside his room. There was a bubble bath awaiting me. The water hot just the way I like it. It was like he was trying to bring me back to life after killing this pussy and ass. He poured me another glass of wine. And feed me the fruit from earlier with added chocolate and crushed nuts. A freak in the bedroom and Martha Steward in the kitchen, shit! That's the type of fuck that had the ability to change your view of things. Like wanting to be cuffed. JK! LMAO! After my bath my body was sleepy but my pussy was awaken. He rolled around in the bed again. We both fell asleep after round 2. I opened my eyes 1st . Watching him sleep photographing his face to my memory. I ran my finger down his face to feel his sexy skin, planted my face between his chin and chest to soak up his scent. I rudely awaken him with my lips wrapped around the snake, let him take me for one last time. Feeling his spirit thru the snake. Hearing his soul thru his fingertips. Seeing his sexy dark chocolate roar. Smelling his sweet freak scent in the air. Tasting his adorable babies. I embodied his essences cause I won't see him again. I could lost myself in him. I just couldn't take that chance. There's a deeper connection between us. Is it love? IDK I'm not prepared for love nor am I willing to love someone other than myself. After he fucked me to sleep for the 3rd time my eyes open with the sun. When the sun has opened its eye but hadn't raised and the sky beam the bright blue. The light shining in from the window ricocheted off the ceiling mirror and tinted the walls and our skin blue. My pussy beaten and battered to the bone but the pleasure written in stone. I've never stayed around long enough to turn blue with anyone but with Bengee it felt true. To be true to my pussy I could turn blue every morning with Bengee. He was perfect roll over dick. LMAO! You know dick that you roll over and get at any time. I left at 5 am. I took a street cab home. I was worn out and need to rest but my mind ran laps around Bengee. UGH!!!! I thought getting his dick in me word get him out of my mind. But it made it worst. FML! I had to get some rest fitness training tomorrow with my MCM of the year in a few hours. LOL! BRB!

Sunday, July 16th

Monday, July 17th

I came home this morning and KO in the living room never even made it to my bedroom upstairs. 15 hours of on and off fucking with Bengee. For the 1st in a long time my pussy was full, burping. LMAO!! No leaking or crying. My whole body wanted to call Bengee and tell him he was the best I ever had but my pride won't let me. Last night while his snake slither through the rivers in my pussy and the mountains in my ass I saw the stars, the moon, the blue sky and sun. I could still taste his loveable babies on my tongue. I couldn't stay in the city today I definitely couldn't trust my pussy now, it was team Bengee. I have never been the cuddling type but I want to be in Bengee arms inhaling his breath. I decided to hop on the metro north horse and ride it to Gucci's crib in Binghamton, after my fitness training with my MCM. I met up with chocolate gladiator with not dick. LMAO! Mr. Marcus Lumar the sexy delicious eye candy met me on 170th street and Highbridge in the BX. Running up and down those 171 steps wore me out. Marcus was standing at the top of the stair looking away. The natural pose made he look like a chiseled muscular statue with the sun beating on his back. The silhouette was amazing. I snapped the pic and posted it on my IG for MCM before he caught me and accuse me of slacking. LOL! I had a work out on top of Bengee's work out. I plan to sleep it off tomorrow. I hopped on the metro north train at Yankee Stadium. As the train rolled on the rails, my mind swayed into reliving the sex-perience with Bengee. I had C breezy blowing in eye thru my headphones. My stomach flipped with butterflies and my pussy cried sweet tears. WOW! Not that some good shit I could come off the thought of Bengee's snake. I was hoping Gucci braided my hair so tight I wouldn't have a thought of Bengee. Gucci was all smile when she picked me up from the train station. I come up twice a month to get my hair done, eyebrows done and re-up on my molly supply, one stop shopping LOL! Gucci had a heavy flow. I was annoyed that she kept taking break to handle BI but none of her clientele was fuck able LOL. JK! She was selling boosted kids clothes, bud and doing my hair. She is true hustler. She finally finished my hair after 5 hours. SMFH! But I was #flawlessonfleek! I loved my new hair so much that we went out to a club. The clubs up here look like down south shacks. The front looks like house. LMAO! It

Monday, July 17th

like somebody knocked out all the walls and made the kitchen a bar. It wasn't really turned up but I made it lit. LOL! Them hick niccas up there ain't never seen ratchet up close, LMAO! I danced on the floor acting a fool with Gucci. Just enjoying her company. Of course niccas was hollering trying to get a selfie, I always show love but tonight I was just Glammaris, not the dancer or the freak. Damn! Can I have a day off? Nicca act like they don't see the curve! Then when you point it out they get tight! FOH! I drank and popped molly to drown out the sound of Bengee's boots from singing in my head and ringing in my pussy. I'm spending the night with Gucci. She had a 5 bedrooms, 3 bathrooms and 2 living rooms. And the kicker is only three people live here, Gucci and her 2 kids. The kids are with their grandparents for the summer. Gucci was happy for the company. Well the sun is coming up. I holla!!! LMAO!!

Tuesday, July 18th

I sleep like infant. I woke up at like 4 in the afternoon. Well rested. I could slightly hear Bengee's boots ringing in my ear. Gucci hostess personality had her make a down south breakfast, grits, scrambled eggs, sausage, waffles, fruit and biscuits. Me and Gucci attack that food like train fighting pit bulls. LMAO! Me and Gucci went to the mall. I was shopping and Gucci was lifting. LMAO. I let her do her thing. I don't fuck around. When we were 17 I went with Gucci to Macy's to get our light finger on and got busted. I was too scared to call my moms. I call Louie grease monkey ass to come get me. I spent 2 bands but we left with 6 bands worth of shit. Gucci had customers lined up. So we swung pass different spots in her sliver X5. After going on Gucci's runarounds we went to the club. I didn't mind doing errands with Gucci. Shit, I got 6 dress, continuous loud cloud following us and all the molly I want all for free. The club was turned up on a Tuesday night and I wasn't being choosey I was going to kill the ringing in my head by having a great time. The manager at the club said if I stay all night I could have free liquor and $500. I don't turn down nothing but my collar. LMAO! I invited Naturel, Cali and Kourtney to join us. Its times like these I really miss Ivory. We took mad pics. While I was just chilling out of nowhere the ringing of Bengee's boots starting ringing in my head. My pussy started humping when this woman walked by. She had Bengee's scent but on a softer side. It was like my nose had put my body in a trance. I started following the woman's scent. My eye spotted the beautiful woman across the dance floor. I said it once and I'll say it again I can admiring a beautiful woman and not hate. IDK if was her cherry red lips or her flawless make-up or her hour glass body wearing the hell out a lace white dress. I went over to only pay her some compliments but my lip's curiosity had a different plan. My innocent human nature of curiosity wanted to know how soft was her skin, how sweet were her lips. Picking up gurls is not what I do! Maybe it was the high, drunk and fucking diet I was on to get Bengee out of my head, kept my heart and mind numb and give the wheel to my pussy. She took my hand and led me to a dark crevice in the club. It was like our minds had the same desires. I tasted her cherry red lips and she tasted my pink cotton candy lips. I kissed the beautiful sexy and sexual woman and I loved it. Her tongue danced around with caring and loving intent in the walls of my mouth. It felt right and wrong, bad and good. It was like I watching my body move. My lips kissed on her neck as her lips copied. I fondled her breast thru the v cut on her dress. I replaced my hands with my lips. She couldn't hold back the moans of pleasure as my tongue taste her nipples. My right hand fingers fondle her pussy in just the right places. Moan and cream gush from her lips. Her cream dripped from my finger on to the floor. I left her standing in the dark corner mind and body confused. It was an experimental game. I have the ability to make a female melt in my hands. LOL! Playing with the woman took my mind of Bengee. I hitched a ride to BK from Kourtney. We laughed and compare this night to many other nights we shared. I was happy to be home. Well I'm going to try on my new shit. BRB!

I woke up at 2 in the afternoon with a down south marching band, drum line in my head. The taste of women's perfume and gold glitter everywhere including my head. I had 2 huge hickies or bruises on my neck and another one on my breast. My mind and my IG have the same pictures. Me booed up with a female. WOW what a hell of a night? I had a great time but it only took the thought of Bengee away for a moment. I need to continue my high, drunk and fucking diet. The diet will keep my heart and mind numb and pussy vivacious and friendly. LOL! My heart and mind wanted to call Bengee. Lie to myself and pretend I could be a part of his world just too lay in his arms one last time. I needed to numb these feelings and thoughts before my body acted on it. I want to tell Bengee exactly how I felt but was afraid of rejection. I posted my WCW! I wish to have her courage. Annalise didn't get away with murdering Americas eyes with her all natural look. LMAO! I envied her courage I want to shed my eyelashes, my make-up, my weave and my lifestyle on Bengee ears. Would he accept me? Would any man? I popped a molly followed by a shot of vodka to take my mind from thinking. I try to scrub the glitter off my skin and shake all thoughts out of my head but not much of it came out. I stopped in the hood to check up on Mr. Buster and Louie. Ran into Earl's ugly ass. I started not to speak. Yeah I'm still tight behind the bullshit at the fight party. Like what nicca run his mouth like a bitch? Why did he have to tell anybody I zoed Jah? Was it anybody's BI? What happened if Jah would have came at me crazy? Earl was screaming niccas was clowning him. So, niccas been clowning him, his whole life! But that day it bothered him? FOH! Miss me with the bullshit! Like really Earl? I wanted to know exactly what niccas were saying "I've giving you mad bread and done made shit for you I should've been got the pussy on a discount, and Jah smashed for 15 hundred "It sound stupid and he looked stupid saying it. So, his come back was Jah got zoed? Wow! He's a fucking dud from getting any more of this here pussy. We go back like cornrow how could he cross me? FOH! I needed to be fucked. Earl's ugly ass had me tight and Bengee had my pussy tight. But I had to hold it down cause I had to go to work. I popped 2 mollys. I started to pop another one when Nicholas showed up as my driver for the evening. Like FOH! Then at work one of my LMS boos got way out of hand.

Wednesday, July 19th

Grab my ass. When I got tight the nicca had the nerve to cuss me out. Calling me, Glammaris, all types of bum bitches, wack pussy bitch, and dick sucking bitch. Straight violated! The deejay stop the music, so the whole fucking club heard him get crazy with me. Talk about being embarrassed! So I throw a drink in his face. I wish his broke ass had a bottle at his table so could've cracked him over the fucking head. Jah stood and watch the whole thing. Jah didn't jump in until the nicca had me by my throat cause my words was eating him alive. I could see it in Jah's eyes, he had heard the rumor that I zoed him. Fucking Earl!!! Aww poor Jah. I should give him back his money or fuck him, right? FOH! HAHA! Playing niccas like sucker!! Instead I caressed Jah's ego with sweet words of confidence. Are you ready for my tight G...I told him "Niccas are going to clown him cause they tight, they wish they could get some of this pussy. It easy for them to believe you got zoed but hard to believe that you actually got the pussy. Don't let these nicca steal you moment to floss what they can't get." When I was done stroking Jah's dick with words off my tongue his chest was pumped up hard. But work is now to be considered unsafe. Jah is a nicca that can't be trusted. SMFH!! I should've worldstar his bitch clown ass, added a little paste around his mouth. LMAO!! I really needed a good fucking, at that point!!! I walked out of the club with my ones in my purse I didn't even cash out. Too much for too little. I went home after work and dolled up and hit a bar in downtown Manhattan, looking for a sex-perience. It was a mix crowd. I had 3 shot of liquor and 2 shots of molly. I was lit and horny. I was dancing all over the place, on the floor, tabletops and on speakers. People could see my underwear, my mini dress was too short to really cover anything, every bend or move had my g-string and pussy were visible. IDGAF! I found myself on the crowded dance floor in the middle of a sandwich. Sexy identical twin brothers, yummy! I was turned on and up by their army fatigues. At 1st I thought I was seeing double. LOL! But one had a Mohawk and one didn't. The Mohawk was behind me. I grind my ass on him while touching on the other one in front of me. Both soldiers were at attention. The DJ made the last call. I bend over and Mohawk couldn't resist sticking his finger in for a feel. Security saw the whole thing and we got kicked out the club for fucking on the dance floor. HA! So I skipped out on my tap LMAO! We were almost out the door when the bartender noticed what had happened. Me and the twin ran for like a block together. It was fun and funny. It was a youthful feeling. Free of adult stress. The twins asked if I was willing to go home with them, they would pay. I would've went with them just not to go home to the conflicting thoughts of Bengee awaiting me but now that money was on the table I was definitely interested. I don't know if it was the 12 body shot I took off the twins 6 pick stomachs, the molly or the Bengee sexual energy but I was sweating bullets. They had a crib walking distance. It felt like I walked miles when it was about 5 city blocks. Once we was inside it got hotter. I walking around their crib butt ass naked like it was my own. Hanging from the chandelier. I was so lit, on that go dumb shit. I was watching my body do these thing but couldn't stop it. There were bottles up but it was going down. LMAO! I was kissing on one brother while the other grind on my ass. With my tongue down his throat I unbutton his pants. My little hands handled his soldier. We moved the party to the Jacuzzi. one brother sat on the edge while I jumped my naked ass in.

Wednesday, July 19th

Mohawk stripped and jumped in the bubbling water with me. I stood between the sitting brother's legs and continue to fondle his standing soldier. The skin was so smooth my tongue begged for a taste. I inhaled his soldier's head and sucked on it like a latex lollipop. The spermicide on the condom numb my mouth I was able deep throat the soldier with no problem. The sucking sound drove Mohawk crazy. Mohawk pull my legs up behind me with him between them. He was holding me like a wheel barrel. He accommodate my wetness with his soldier. With one brother plunging his gun down my esophagus and Mohawk pumping machine gun shots in my intestines it felt like their heads were bumping inside my body. They held my body above the water but the bubbles were grazing my stomach it tickled and aroused me at the same time. They were identical in looks, stokes and timing. They came at the same time. We switched positions. I had my back against the Jacuzzi's wall and Mohawk was standing over me probing my mouth with his soldier and the brother was between my legs grilling his solider in my rectum. I wanted to scream out the pleasure that hurt so good with the strong shot to my rectum but my throat was clogged with shot of cream. The other brother had freed his soldier from the wrap of my tongue and the latex. He jerked his soldier until it spit out the eye into mouth. The creamy saliva from the soldier over flowed from my mouth running down cheeks and chin. Mohawk shouts as his soldier shots off in the latex inside my rectum. They had cum together again. I collected my 12 hundred and got into the cab that they called for me. I just got inside my brownstone and its 5 in the morning and I noticed my dress is torn and I lost my bra! I wanted to say that playtime with the twins, Wayne and Sean. Sean has the Mohawk or is it Wayne with the Mohawk? IDK! LMAO! But the twins did take my mind of Bengee but the clicking of their dog tags reminded me of the sweet chime of Bengee boots. I'm beat and Thursday has just begun it 10 am. I had a long night! LOL! Well let me post my TBT pic before I KO! I'm posting a pic of all of us Cali, Gucci, Ivory, Kourtney, Naturel, and myself. Me and Cali are the same age and the youngest out the group. Gucci is now 31 yrs. old, the oldest. Ivory, Kourtney and Naturel in middle at the same age. The pic was taken when Gucci made us all start speaking again. I'm going to put you on right quick. This lame XL nicca named Gello, use to always try to holler at me but I dub him each and every time. At 15 yrs old I didn't have time for charity work! I was try to get my coins up. 1st off he was a BBD lame XL nicca aka **broke, busted disgusting**, a unknown, and fat! FOH!!!! I didn't want to be seen even talking to him. The next year Gello got his coins up and hollered at Cali. He was tricking really good on Cali. one day he ran down on me like "I'm up now, so can you go down?" I topped him of for 200 and a pair of J's, and everybody came crashing down on me like I fucked Cali's main, like I took bread out her hand. The nicca was and is a fucking dollar to both of us! Why would she care? We don't love them hoes! LMAO! I've passed the drop on plenty of niccas. You think I was in the wrong or agree with me no harm no foul? But my move had divided the group for a minute and Gucci killed the beef and took this pic in remembrance of the reunion. I posted the pic from 5 yrs ago side by side with the pic we took the other night, remember? I can no longer keep my eye lids open. TTLY

Friday, July 21st

Yesterday was one of the worst days of my life. SMFH! I can't believe I sleep Thursday way like that? It was fucking 7 pm when I opened my eyes. WOW! I guess the twin wore me out more then I remembered! LMAO! I sat in my living room on top of the brick red rug in front of the fireplace and counted out 1,086 singles, not bad for a Wednesday night. I was having a drink as my mind sipped on Wednesday night's fuckery with one of my LMS boos and Jah clown ass. Why niccas and bitches think they can say whatever they want to me? Yes, I fuck and suck dick all day and I'm a stripper but before all of that I am human! It crazy how the people have double standards. Men runaround here humping on anything moving and they get praises from his bros and more pussy from the women that have heard or seen how they serve it up. But when I do it I'm looked upon as the lowest being on earth. Men don't have a problem with my lifestyle until I say no then I'm being called out off my name. Like really? I was the baddest chick you ever saw just a second ago, now I don't want to take a pic, fuck or suck your dick now I'm all type of bitches, hoes and smuts. Miss me with the bullshit. Then follow the bitches judgmental rumors. #one trending topic: Glammaris pussy! "her pussy got to be stretched out." FOH Bitches! Every nicca you see me with on the gram isn't getting a cut. Excuse me bitches but we get the same amount of dick. Bitches fuck their man, boo, or whatever every night, and I fuck a different nicca every night. Same difference. Bitches be killing me!!! Watch what's coming in and out your man's pockets and not what's cumming in and out my pussy cause I'm going to get paid! LMAO!! I took my time getting ready for work last night. I really didn't want to go back there the vibe is so off. My driver was Nicholas again, SMFH. As soon as I walking in the club Sugar was all in my face about the fucking medical form. Like seriously? Who the fuck do she think she is, co-owner? She should breathe when sucking Black's dick the lack of oxygen to her brain didn't have her thinking straight, talking to me like that. Black came out of the shadows backing her words. WOW! Is it ever that serious to actually rundown yelling and violating my personal space over a fucking medical form? I want to slap Black's lips off his face and spit in Sugar's eye and watch her melt for snickering in the background. But I'M FUCKING GLAMMARIS! Black wasn't going to stand in the way of my paper! But the nicca dead ass wouldn't let me enter the club without the form. I was embarrassed 2 nights in row. I was so fucking tight. So I walked out of the club with my head held high but I felt low. I was standing outside the club waiting for my car to pull up, Jah brings his clown ass outside talking about I had to leave the premises. His smile glowing from his yellow teeth. He was happy to try to play me. I told Jah to suck my pussy and eat my ass! FOH! My fingers couldn't dial Naturel's number fast enough. My hands were shaking I was so mad. I needed and wanted to know what the fuck is going on? Black was so extra with his shit and he was flossing Sugar like she had Naturel's spot. She answered sobbed in the phone "Glammaris, I'm so... sorry, please forgive me." and hung up. What's with the extras tonight! I try calling her back several times. I could find another strip club to work at, she shouldn't be weeping. LMAO! So fried! But she never answered the phone again. I sent out texts to all the gurls to meet at my crib. We got to get Naturel off the Black's dick drug ASAP! I had the night to myself since I couldn't work. SMFH! I remember bar hopping with some cool ass chicks I meet at one of the bars. Then I followed them to someone's crib. They say never drink with a heavy heart or mind. Well both my heart was burden with thoughts of Bengee and my mind was so tight with Black, Jah and Naturel bitch asses. I worked 3 yrs at that club and he handle me like a bitch of the street. All the times that I've listen to him cry over Naturel's pussy I thought we had some type of rapport, I guess I was wrong! SMFH! I popped molly and floated on loud clouds with the cool but strange females I meet. I woke up this morning in a strangers bed, with a belly piercing, and a tattoo on my right waist that say WHY NOT and a missing eyebrow, I'm talking waxed completely off! I had a sour taste in my mouth from sipping on that lean. Lean was cough syrup with a splash of codeine mixed with soda. My pussy's monthly volcano erupted on my white pompom shorts. I crawled out of the stranger's bed without awaking the stranger and fled the crime scene. Whoever he is, he going to be tight when he wakes up and see that cherry puddle in his bed. Embarrassing!!! I called the car service from the lobby. I had to take one of the stranger's sweaters to cover up the lava over flow. I flew in the car. Nicholas was the driver. I have never been happy to see him before today. I prayed Tau didn't show. Whew!!! This was some fucking week. I had spent my days locked in a haze and mind amazed by fazes at night. High, drunk and fucking diet heart numb but pussy pumping. Only made me want Bengee even more. I need real down time just to think things over. I looked through my phone pics to restore my mind about last night as I sat in the backseat. It appears I had plan on getting a tat on my face. That explains my missing eyebrow. But my throw up on the tattoo artist ended the session. LMAO! I took a bath and a nap. Swept in and out of the hood, to check up on Mr. Buster and pick up from grease monkey Louie, who was short $100, craps was too bad to really beef and was back home. I fell out in the living room on the cappuccino colored chaise in front of the window. I was woken up by the gurls arrival. Everybody showed up but Naturel. Everybody that comes to my brownstone falls in love with rooftops. I must admit its fire! Even more so after add artificial palm trees, I had too after being in Miami. LMAO! They shared their cocktales over cocktails but I was silent. I was hiding my missing eyebrow with a Yankee fitted that I copped just to remember Mr. Yankee fitted, from ATL. LMAO! My situation couldn't be verbalized to their understanding. Shit, I was confused. Even if I told them I thought I was in love they wouldn't believe me much less listen to me. But I honestly feel it in my heart that I was in love with Bengee. But my pussy was still in love with fucking. SMFH!!! Most bitches have 99 problems, all I had was one, my pussy. My heart couldn't ctrl my pussy and my pussy couldn't ctrl my heart, they had to different agendas. Many would say just settle with Bengee but TBH I love the whole lifestyle of it all. Robbing a nicca with words or profiling a nicca and frisking his pockets with this here pussy LMAO! I don't think I could ever give it up. Some like bike riding, horseback riding, surfing or rock climbing, but I love riding dick. It sooo much fun. LMAO! And each any every men or nicca have their own unique style of fucking that influence a different sexual pleasure in me. When the dick is in my hand or in my pussy it have complete power over me and each sex-perience is a different pleasure. The pleasure is manifested in my speech and my actions in the heated moments. They were talking I was half listening to them and the half listening to my heart. But when their conversation curved and they were talking about Naturel's cocktales, labeled as a "situation." I was all ears. Gucci laid it all out by saying "She needs to let Black old ass go especially after he throw her out. Niccas love to show their ass. I been telling her get her own out of his ass. She better get that bun out the oven. Y'all know how it is when that alone time is essential to discovering self, healing and planning how to move forward. Let at her stay at her Auntie's house in Jersey, she'll come back. That's when our friendship is going to be needed." I know exactly what Naturel was going through. I had to run to get thru this sick feeling in my stomach that just won't stop, it was a bunch of questions I swallowed that wasn't agreeing with my insides. I wanted bomb Bengee with questions relating to his vision for us. I know he wanted something more than sex-perience, I felt it and I know he felt it too. SMFH!!! What am I going to do? Back to Naturel! WOOOW! Pregg? Wow! The story they was discussing was missing pieces I could tell by the puzzled look on their faces. Like I knew 1st hand Black wanted Naturel knocked up so why would he throw her out? They was holding back key parts. Something was going on with Naturel.

I soon find out but now I had to find my way. I don't know how but the words swayed toward Earl ugly ass. Apparently he has been crying to Cali his apologies but betrayal is wrong that could never be right. And he was blind to his wrong cause he was still doing it. Running his fucking mouth. Got them questioning the depth of our friendship. FOH! Earl is so fried and a dub! The gurls just left. I had to grab my notebook and free the words sitting on my stomach. Women need a place where we can speck freely about our sex-periences without out the fear of the labels being slapped on our skin. I know I'm not alone but we would never know cause of the hidden fear. There's plenty of other women that feel and think the way I do but would never act on it and can't never talk about. Where do we go? Shit I wish I could sit down with a cocktail and tell a real cocktale like Mr. Yankee fitted. LMAO!!! Wow Will Smith's words just popped in my head. "Glammaris Cocktales" so delicious they "Change the world." An open forum were all women can speak without the shackles of ugly labels on beautiful women. I wonder how many secrets lives in the dirty and urn? Women who have expired being prisoners of their sex-perience. Well I'm going to holler in a few days. These craps, belly piercing, heartache, headache, pussy lava, tattoo and a waxed eyebrow all was throbbing in unisons. When I get my monthly eruption not only does my pussy self-cleanse so do my whole body, I'm talking shits and vomit. I looked in my body size mirror. I still had the 2 huge hickies or bruises on my neck and the other one on my breast. And about 3 more from sliding down the pole at work. Bags under my eyes from the overdosing on alcohol, molly and sexy. TTYL! ☹ ☹

Did you miss me? I'm back @ 100% LMAO! My pussy's lava has stop flowing and my pussy was growling like a caged dog. It's been a 5 days since I had dick and the last time is fuzzy in my memory. SMFH! I'm kinda feeling the "Why Me?" tat. The belly piercing grow on me too. It kinda sexy. LMAO! My eyebrow is actually growing in and the bruises wore out. I still had heartache over Bengee but I'm getting thru it. SMFH! Well here's the drop. Saturday and Sunday I half laid in my queen size bed watching ratchet reality TV and the other half running to the bathroom to either shit or vomit, detoxing from every hole, no pause, LMAO! Wait til I tell you this… the mailman was banging down my front door Monday afternoon interrupting my MCM post. Because I had pussy lava pouring I cancelled my fitness training with Marcus. I posted the king snoop lion. Cause he made the world accept him for who he is, smoker with blue rag hanging from the left side of his back pocket. #SALUTES to the king of change! The mailman was very young to be delivering mail. He said 23 but looked 15. My taste buds was barking at him but I didn't want to sic my tongue on him, LOL. He delivered a large green box. I ripped through to see what was inside. Whenever I get a gift I turn in to 8 yrs. old on Christmas morning. LMAO! I couldn't believe it! I was selected for Emery's trophy. AAAAH!!! A pair of Giuseppe heels with white wings, retail value $1595. With an invitation to a meeting on the 31st @ the Empire State building, 36th floor, @ 9am. I was dumb hyped. I wonder what states I'll get to explore. How long is the tour? And most importantly how much was the tour paying? I picked up my phone to call Earl but realized I wasn't talking to him. I felt like Ivette when she was waiting on Baby boy and realized she had the keys in her purse. I missed my friend. Yeah I fucked Earl ugly ass from time to time but our conversations were more intimate. ☹ I turned to music to fill Earl's absents. Yesterday I went to my doctor's appointment. I'm STD free. I already knew that cause I be packing rubbers in all sizes LMAO! And I'm in good health. I can't wait to go to work tonight and throw my form in Black's mouth. Vanilla, a dancer, at club texted me and told me all the shit he was flushing out his mouth about me. Like I was his example of not following the rules. FOH! And fuck Black! I got 30 bands tucked in a safe in my closet's floor. I'm so good. Gabe came creeping in the door like a husband sneaking in from staying the night out. He wasn't he usual self he was shaky like he was hiding something. He was talking a lot but wasn't saying nothing. I told him I love him, when I didn't, to fuck him. I told him it was his pussy, when it wasn't, so he fuck harder. When we were done he started his pity party BS. I decided at that moment Gabe was more trouble then his worth. He could lay it down but he didn't beat it up and he whine to much like a true bitch nicca. The past is gone I can't change or fix it and I refuse to keep reliving it. I can't apologize for being a fucking monster, literally. I have accepted me a long time ago, Gabe and other people have to catch up. I took the keys to my Brownstone off his chain and took the pity out my heart. I kicked Gabe ass out and close the door on that part of my life. I handle him with cold hands cause I try to keep him warm with this pussy fitting like a glove and he still was unhappy. FOH! Gabe put me in an ode shabby mood and my pussy in thirst mood, he watered it but didn't quench the thirst. Bengee texted me today and my heart texted back. I still wasn't ready to face Bengee or the feelings beating fast in my chest. I called the car service, Tau was the driver, yummy! I keep my hands, mouth and pussy to myself. He dumped me off in the hood. I went to check up on Mr. Buster and the grease monkey. I'm not going to hold you up, my pussy was looking for Earl but I was extra low key about it. When I didn't bump in to Earl I took a cab home and called Tau over. Before he arrived I ran down to the studio apartment with some things from my house to give it that "lived in" interior decorating, LMAO! While I waited for Tau my ears listened to the pink print and my heart eavesdropped on the blue print of me and Earl's connection drawn with life events. The ups like my 1st pair of TRUs or the juicy necklace and bracelet set that I wanted more than air to breathe, it was Earl who got it for me. The downs, Earl literally fighting niccas in the street. his fist against the rumors and facts crowded around my pussy. Or our biggest fight, when were 16 that ended with blood shed. These is how it went down. I was in puppy love with Reinaldo Walker. Back then every nicca I fucked with had to be cool with Earl cause he was always with me. Earl was security on deck. LMAO! Bitches always trying to rundown but got ran up on by Earl. FOH! They were tight!!! Any way back to the drop. Reinaldo fucked a bitch while chilling with Earl.

Earl came back and told me but left out that he give Reinaldo the assumption that we had something without words but with a facial expression. I was so mad at Reinaldo and Earl but Earl was the only one around so I took all my hurt out on him. In the mist of the word battle between us he called me a smut. And I swung a knife and cut him. I was so sorry right after I did it. We were in the ER for 10 hours and when we left Earl had 20 stitches on the back of his right forearm. All of my life memories are filled with images of Earl. I have a scar on my right knee, from when I was in 3rd grade I fell during recess while playing baseball with the boys and scraped off skin and meat of my knee. Earl took me to the nurse and stood there and waited there until he was forced back to class. Or when I fell off my bike at 12 yrs. old and had to get 3 stitches under my chin. It was Earl who was by my side in the ER with my parents. My mind flipped thru my timeline memories. Just like Gabe, Earl is someone I have to let go. And it's going to be hard but they will never hold my heart the way I touch theirs. It's wrong for me to stand in their way of what they real want and would never get from me. I posted Nicki as my WCW, not cause she beautiful and successful but cause she share all sides of her personality and world has embraced it. Freedom of self, #SALUTE! Tau showed up with wine and flowers in his hands. His smile turned upside down from the sight of water under my eyes. He had arrived while I was playing the crying game with emotions. But I cleaned up and change the mood and my outfit. My pussy had a taste for foreign exotic dark chocolate. The plan was to get drunk and forget what we did but 1st I had to deal with Black's ass. I ran up in the club with Tau's African blood diamond frame in my shadow. I marched right into his office. Interrupted Sugar sucking his dick and pockets dry at the same time. I through the form in his face and quit. "I'm sorry Glammaris! You friend hurt me and I took it out on you cause I felt like you know what was going on behind my back and smiling in my face." Is what he said I had no clue of what he was talking about, so I questioned him. "The nicca she was fucking got her pregnant not me, the nicca Gabe!" I asked him to repeat himself cause I couldn't be hearing right. Yup he said Gabe. Tau took me home my stomach was upset, heart hurting and pussy turned off. I gave at Tau a fucking rain check. I'm playing the emotional crying game again. ☹ ☹ ☹ GTG!

Thursday, July 27th

Good morning, ☺ I feel much better, I'm still hurting but feeling better. Pussy back to purring LMAO! I'll talk about it on these pages but never from my lips. Ok I get that they both "TRY" to tell me. Remember Naturel's "I'm sorry over the phone? And Gabe stumbling over his words before I shut him up with putting my pussy in his mouth. But neither one of them actually told me. So I called Cali last night and she spilled it all. Gucci wanted only Naturel to tell me and nobody else, all the gurls agreed. Cali said it was a late night thirsty moment and nothing more. Gabe came to my brownstone I wasn't home but Naturel was there. Ok, so am I crazy or do you see the disrespect? 1st off Gabe ain't some nicca I'm jerking for chicken. At one point in my life I did loved him and Naturel knows that. And on top of that she fucked him in my crib. Straight violation! That's why I rarely fuck with bitches they always over step the line. And Gabe been laying down past guilt strong on me when his present innocent was in question. These hoes ain't loyal! I guess I wasn't supposed to feel no kinda way cause I don't want Gabe but he was still mine. SMFH! I wanted to call Earl and hear his take on the BS but couldn't. I posted my TBT pic of me and

Thursday, July 27th

Earl 15 yrs. old smoking in the staircase. I'm smiling from ear to ear I was so happy to be me, not like now where I feel like I'm always defending me. I'm having a spa day and lite shopping spree, the best therapy ever. I got to get my game face on for Ivory's birthday party tomorrow. ☹ I can't let them know I rubbed by this BS. But I would love to have 2 minutes of Naturel's time. TTLY. ME TIME BEGINS NOW!!! LOL!!

My nails is done, got my hair curled, bought some expensive fabric and had a full body massage, it wasn't the Earl special ☹ but the best money could buy. Bengee's text said he wanted to meet up tonight. My pussy wanted to jump out at the opportunity but my heart wasn't ready to let him into my pussy without getting involved. All I had left to do was take care of my crying pussy. I dolled up and slipped into my DTF dress. LMAO! Yes Nicholas puck ass was the driver but IDGAF! My pussy had an agenda, I didn't mind paying. I popped a molly in he back seat before entering the bar. As soon as I entered the dim lit bar on the Upper East Side there was a set of eyes undressing me. Staring at me pass 3 seconds meant he wanted to either

Thursday, July 27th

fight or fuck, let a this nicca try me I going to fuck around a catch a body. LMAO! He invited himself over to sit at the bar with me. From his side grin I could tell he didn't want to fight. LOL! I had my ass hanging off the stool and my arms folded on the bar's wooden counter, teasing the eyes with the sex-tra arch in my back. He was handsome and had to be wealthy or just stunning. The way he was throwing cash around. He dared me to kiss another chick in the bar for a band doubting my freakiness. Easy money, I sobbed her down like she was my wife for yrs. LMAO! He couldn't wait to see me strip and I couldn't wait to see how smooth he flowed out of them clothes. I was super turned up it was my 1st molly in 6 days he was going to get a hell of an sex-perience tonight. LMAO! In every nicca or man I meet I was searching for part of Bengee in them. Well this nicca was rocking Bengee's scent that had my heart and pussy wide open. Thoroughbred animalistic hood nicca, named Noah. He wasted no time as soon as we got to the hotel room he turned up. His ark ready for sailing. A hardcore beat that I could dance too. The hood in him fucked me in different variation of doggy style. onest I was on both knees, then on one and then on none supporting my body with my forearms. He power drove his hood dick in my watering pussy. I bounced my ass fast but shook it slow. The more I took that flow of the ark the harder it sailed. I was rocking the boat with the heavy creamy waves. He sink his ark deeper into the waves. From hard to slow. He stuck with his doggy style theme and made me stand on my weak legs. His hood Ark traveled to the ghetto of my soul. He rock my hips while I bit my lip. His hand lift my left leg off the floor and held my thigh up in left hand. The strokes came at rapid speed. I stood on my tippy toes on my right foot taking the crashes of ark against my waves. My creamy tears of pleasure was streaming down his leg. He was killing this pussy until his ark hit a rock of pleasure. The ark gushed in to the latex. My pussy walls felt the cream pumping out the ark's hole. Shit that what I am talking about a nicca that can handle driving a boat. He had severed his purpose. He was a breath of fresh air to my congested thoughts. I skipped out while he was sleeping. My flexibility always stretch nicca out. LMAO! They should thank my moms for her lumber limbs or maybe it's the practice I got sliding down the project heating piles as a kid. LML!

Thursday, July 27th

The projects bred stripper! I left while he was sleep I didn't want to ruin the moment with a curve. I'm home now going to shower and sleep until the party tomorrow. I wonder it Earl, Gabe and Naturel going to show up? TTYL

This morning I woke up with my pussy on hell of thirsty, LOL! Noah was a nice ride but I needed a roller coaster. I wanted to twerk my pussy while in a slit on some dick. Body rocking, booty popping from the bumps or a roller coaster ride. LMAO!! My mouth really want a taste of that Aone sauce from Mr. Yankee fitted. HA! And I ain't talking steak, I'm talking pure southern beef. LOL! These are the times I think about Bengee the most. I want to rollover in the middle of the night onto his crawling snake. I wanted to drink his protein shake for breakfast. He wanted me as much as I wanted him, I know from his text convo. We text back and forth often, at least once a day casual texts but I could read between the letters. So out of boredom I set an IG thirst trap, LMAO! I posted a pic of my ass and converted it to pencil sketch with the caption, "Who wanna paint me white?" LMAO! Niccas went ham on the gram. Their snouts had them commenting all types of craziness. The DM's started flowing in like a tide, LMAO! I give some of them credit, they had heart, cause I wouldn't sent a pic of my little piglet tail to anybody's DM. Like what if I expose them and posted their 2 by 2 dick on the gram. LMAO!!! Shit got more crazy. LMS

Friday, July 28th

niccas were arguing with each other in the comments. It was funny but like word on my fucking pic? LMS niccas! Like one had a chance over another. LMAO!! I thought pigs had a heighten sense of smell? How come they didn't smell that thirst trap? LMAO!! You know the hating ass bitches commented the usual, "THOT" in different variation with and or without the "bitch", "dirty", "stank pussy" and "stretch out pussy." Like seriously? You come to my page to call me names, who is the real loser in this story? SMFH! Bitches hate me cause they want to be me. I don't mean it in a conceited tone. I mean it like they wish they could live life with sex-perience like I do. But their name calling don't do shit to me!!! Their words don't take no food out my mouth or chicken out my pocket, or dick out my pussy, I stay full like I just ate. LMAO!!! I was being entertain by the negative attention as well as the positive, but my pussy was not! And it happened right on cue, Chipy texted me, right when my pussy was getting agitated. I could never forget his complexion of a perfectly baked cookie, not too dark and not too light, from the 1st time I lined him at Emery's 4th of July party. His eyebrows like plush velvet over sliced almond shaped eyes, long seductive eye lashes, a quarter size brown mole on his left cheek looked like a chocolate chip. The multi sized speckles of chocolate chips all over his 5"8 frame in length and something like 50 cent width. I like fucking Chipy's Pillsbury cookie dough roll. It's fun to milk his lack of skills to my advantage and we both eat, me and my pussy. Last time, he almost had it. He had my feet praying to the hotel ceiling. LMAO!! He was feeling himself this morning. He must've tested his cooking skills I taught him with his cookie dough on an easy bake oven and thought he could fuck with this Brick oven. The temperature in a brick oven can't be controlled. LMAO! He had my band and the $100 he shorted me last time. It was early when all this texting was going on. I had time to take a bite out of Mr. Tough cookie and collect my coins. Come back home shower and be on time for the party. I wonder how the party decorations looks, Naturel bitch ass punked out on doing the decorations and entertainments. She is really running like we weren't never friends. She could ask to live in my brownstone several times but couldn't talk to me? Straight running, for what? Don't get me wrong I am mad. I just want to know what's her next move? Is she going to keep it? I really want to know what's emotions are rolling around in her mind? She pass the party duties off to Gucci and Kourtney. I called the car service of course Tau is the driver. WTF! I didn't want to curve him but I already had a taste for a cookie, not chocolate. Plus Tau's exotic chocolate is my favorite snack. LMAO! I want to curl up with the chocolate snack and nibble on him during a movie night. Shit, it's an art too taking all that big foreign dick, it should be documented, LMAO!!! But this morning wasn't his turn. Aww Tau had the sad puppy eyes. All niccas no matter the race or age always get sensitive over this pussy. I'm not being arrogant I promise! It's just undisputable! I popped a molly in the back seat. I really didn't need to pop the little crystal cause my pussy was clearly turned up of the wake up. I try to pay Tau but he didn't want my money he wanted me to spend time. I had to breezy on him. His sad eyes was sparking a nerve in me. Chipy was ready to go when I entered the hotel room on the 10th floor on west 59th street. He ripped my clothes off. He push me up against the wall and lift my thighs to his waist. "You ready to take this dick?" yes I was. He was being aggressive the way I am to him. And I was being the passive one like he was under my hostile pussy. From the wall to the floor he feed my pussy. His cookie dough roll was hitting all the right spots. With my back against the carpet and my ankles folded behind his head he was dipping his cookie dough deep into my milking creamy pussy. I drop my legs down and planted my feet on the carpet. My pussy wanted to fight back. His cookie dough was cooking my pussy. I couldn't let Chipy get the best of me. Before I could settle into position to toss this pussy on him. He had lift me up and laid me out on the bed. He stood up on the side of the bed. "Stop, running from this dick!" The words alone coming from his lips made my pussy milked. He then grabbed my ankles and held them in the air after he guided his dough into my milky pussy. He was beating up my pussy but it hurt so good. I gave my pussy a break and tasted the cookie dough dipped in cream. The combination of the two creams on my taste buds was a supernatural taste charge with sex-cellent lust. I licked it up. My greedy pussy cried for another taste of the cookie dough. I laid back down on the bed from sitting position. He bent my legs forward, my knees to my breast. He use his left hand to

Friday, July 28th

escort the dough into my awaiting milking pussy.
His pelvic thrust was earth moving. "You taught
me well, huh? Got you running from this dick." I
was gripping the pillow with my teeth. He pull
me up to sitting position. My lips and tongue was
devouring the cookie dough. His cookie crumbed
with cream. The cream slide down my tities. He
spank my lips with the dough. I gave him a high
5. I was proud he could finally work his tool. He
was so sex-cited we went a congratulation
round. LOL! I took a cab off the street back to
my brownstone, didn't want to look at Tau's sad
eyes. I was thinking about Chipy on the ride
home. I wasn't going to see him again. He was
going after his girl and I encouraged it. I was
happy I could help him. Now he can go get his
girl back from the nicca that stole her. People
only see the "bad" and is blind to the good I do.
So what I charged him! The game is always too
be sold and never just told. I had the itis and a
stomachache from taking all that cookie dough.
LMAO! I got up from my nap and started
getting ready for the party at around 7pm my
pussy was quiet but my mind was screaming
Bengee. It was like the thought of him just
linger around in my head all day every day.
SMFH! I popped another molly in my mouth and

sipped on my alcohol mix "*Glammaris Cocktale.*" I keep it simple a peach colored maxi fitting dress with the little sandals I got from Tricky Nicky, at the private "yacht" party, in Key West, remember? I wonder what Snowflake is up too? I keep in contact with April. Missy is doing a photo spread in Canada as I write, for a swimsuit company. She was super happy when I told her I was selected trophy for Emery. I beat my face and laid my hair. #spiralcurlsonfleek! I was fashionably late, LOL!! I like being the last one to show up. All eyes on me not my eyes on everybody. The gurls hooked the roof top basketball court up. Coach Scott only stuck around to see me walk in, he then disappeared. Instead of the bleachers all being on the left side of the roof top, they were split in half. one on each end of the court, both of them facing half court. All types of food, cupcakes, sodas and the huge basketball going through the rim cake was dressing the table on the sidelines. The color theme was blue and yellow to match the colors painted on the basketball court. There were blue and yellow balloons and streamers everywhere. It was cute. I greeted the gurls, Cali, Gucci and Kourtney, they was surrounding the birthday girl. When I pulled up on them, I could feel the Gabe and Naturel situation was on their lips. They questioned my emotional status, as if I should be broken down. I've said it before I'm hurt, mad and disappointed in both of them but broken down, NAH! I passed off Ivory her birthday gift, it was a bag of all different types of brand names and brand new quality perfumes along with the grease monkey's 200 dollars. I had stopped by Louie's to get my weekly pick-up, LOL! I was sitting quietly in the corner enjoying the show. Friends I haven't seen in years, some grown into different types of success. And friends who have grown but still planted in the same spot. Kourtney's man works at Madison square garden, he's the reason the Harlem Globetrotters were performing. Ivory love Basketball she was smiling from ear to ear. All her family, friends, doctors and nurse were in attendance. It was a nice turn out. I was fucking up the game. I had 2 bitches and a groupie at the party. SMFH! Earl ugly ass and Gabe slimy ass are the bitches and Elton is the groupie. Earl was like my shadow following me around asking the same question in different ways. I said "No I didn't fuck Elton" a 100 times, in a 100 different words but Earl didn't hear me once. Gabe begging for forgiveness. I try to pick his brain about Naturel. But he didn't know nothing, so I had nothing else to say to him. And Elton, please have some dignity. BRAH! This your BM party like show so type respect for her cause his was gone! SMFH! I should've never let him drive me too work, now he feeling like he got a shot at scoring some of this there pussy. His nose wide open off the scent of the pussy. DAMN! And the worst of it all, he is doing it out in the open. I'm a bitch for half egging it on with flirtatiously flipping of my eyelashes and playful taps to his chest and shoulder. My interaction with Elton was eating Earl from the inside out. Earl was looking so hard his neck had to be broke from all that rubber necking. LMAO! Earl ugly face was boxed up, his hanging lips curled with jealousy and his gremlin textured hands balled up into a fist. He looked like an ugly kid trying to hold back tears. LMAO! The deejay was killing the speakers with 90's music. I was dancing around with Cali. It funny how music can transport the mind to the past. Me, Cali, Gucci and Ivory was remising on memorable moment we shared, the niccas we zoed and bitches that hated us. Then the unthinkable happened. Earl walked over to me and got down on one knee and proposed marriage. "I've been in love with since I was 8 yrs. old. I want to spend the rest of my life by your side, as husband and not as your friend." I wanted to kick his teeth down his throat and hoped he choked to death. Earl use to be my favorite cause he spoke freak silently. It's clear we don't speak the same language any more. SMFH! I was so mad. Not only was he announcing his love publicly but he was lowering the value of my pussy from caviar and champagne to nuggets and soda. I came to the party willing to kill the tiff with Earl but now he was a complete dub! I said "HELL NO!" maybe if he would of done it privately I would've accepted his 5/8 cut diamond, supported by plenty of tiny diamonds on the strawberry 14 kt gold band. The pink gold was beautiful. I envisioned it on my finger while it was in the box. The ring had to cost him at least 5 bands easy. I hated Earl for this. Everybody on the roof top had a puzzled faces. I could read the questions in their eyes. Cali couldn't bit her tongue she ask straight out "You been fucking ugly Earl all these years?" Gabe had the "I know it!" look in his eyes. I can't begin to write the endless argument between me and Gabe over

Friday, July 28th

Earl throughout the yrs. I wanted to put hand, feet and violent words on Earl but didn't want to cause a scene. So I grabbed Elton by the hand and lead him to a Janitor's closet, by my movements I was ripping Earl's heart right out his chest. Earl had ruin a 15 yrs of friendship by straight up exposing our secret to everyone. News by mouth get around faster than news on any channel. I gave Elton what he was begging for all night. My pussy refused to hump his below average dick. He wanted a taste and a mouthful is what he got. He was speaking in tongue while committing the ultimate sin. Elton had looks but no dick. God, gave all the dick to Earl, LOL! He had no choice but to jerk his own dick off, my little hand were too big. LOL! I went in the closet angry and came out of the closet ashamed. The looks on Earl and Ivory face hit my heart. SMFH! I ran out the party and took a cab off the street home. Yes I was ducking Tau. I couldn't take another disappointing look tonight. I have a river of confused feelings flowing from my eyes. I was really mad that I didn't stay to the end. I wanted to see if Naturel was going to show her face. GTG!

Saturday, July 29th

I woke up with puffy eyes and a sore heart. I truly wanted to see Bengee. When I'm in his presence it's peaceful, playful, and sex-ceptional. I called Ivory last night to offer apologizes and lunch this afternoon. She insisted that there was no apology needed and declined on lunch. She was over Elton yrs. ago and didn't care who pussy he slurped on. But I could still hear her disappoint in my value of our friendship. She also mention Naturel never showed face at the party. Earl and Elton was taking her daughter to their family reunion in Philly. When she mentioned the family reunion my memory flashed to Earl asking me to accompany him to the fun-ction. I was happy to hear my pussy didn't standing in between their brotherhood, thank God! I'm so mad at Earl. Having Elton eat my pussy and toss my salad in the closet didn't give fulfillment to his injuries for scabbing my image. I wanted to inflict pain and suffering to him. SOOOOOO OUT OF LINE! I just was feeling all types of ways. I called Tau over. Chocolate is my favorite comfort snack. I let Tau come into where I really live. He took a look at me and saw right through me. Tau wanted to take care of me and I let him. He set up a bubble bath for me. I uses my right hand to hold his left hand for balance as I stepped into the bubbles of warm water. I settled my body into the water and exhaled heavy. Tau picked up my pink face cloth off the bathroom sink. He rinsed the face cloth out in the bathroom sink. He lathered up soap on the face cloth. He kneeled down on the side of the bathtub. He folded the face cloth in a smaller square. I watched him move with such poise. His movement was like he was gracefully dancing to music. He gently passed the soapy face cloth across my forehead, down my left cheeks, to my chin. He performed the same technique to the right side of my face. He used the face cloth to clean the corners of my eyes, nose and lips. He had freed my face from all makeup and my emotions dissembled. I started thinking out loud. Telling Tau the whole story behind Gabe and Naturel. I was mad but how could I hold a grudge when I just did the same exact thing to Ivory? Minus the pregnancy. I just wanted to know was she going to keep it, if not, I wanted to be there for her like she was for me! I told how I wanted to rock Earl's ring on my finger and fuck the shit out of Bengee with my heart at the same time. My love for Tau's catering touch rolled off my tongue. I don't think I'm greedy for share my pussy with each of these men for different reason. I had a different type of emotional connection with these men and I wasn't ashamed of it or ashamed of being me! Either was ashamed of the other sex-periences I had. Sucking Mr. Buster's soggy dick was help a soul in need. I like slurping on the sponge texture of the last captain crunch floating around in the cereal bowl. My taste buds has falling in love with Mr. Yankee fitted A1 sauce. There was something in the ingredients that made me crave it. I was truly amazed by my skills, putting Christopher Peterson in a pussy choke hold until he fall asleep, teaching Chipy how to handle his tool like a G and making a ballerina out of West. Sucking on Ock's uncircumcised dick that smell like old hot dog water, his cottage cheese smelling belly rubbing the top of my weave had unbeatable benefits. I love feeding Coach Scott "In love with the coco" white man fetch with my pussy. I Like bouncing Tyree young ass around with my pussy while I breastfeed him my nipples. I love having it go up on Tuesday by tonguing a chick down in the club while rubbing her clit. I love having a sex-cellent time with twins. It was pure fun zoeing Jah or leaving the dreadlock photographer in the club like a rape victim. I love following Bengee's scent into Noah's arms. I love finagling words so men and niccas dance to my beat while they greased my pockets, LOL! TBH,I love this shit and everything that come with the clothes, bags, hair, life style, money, nails and of course the dick. If being me makes me a thot then THOT LIFE IT IS!!!! #thottyhotty! No I didn't have some horrible experience as a child. I just love dick. Tau words of acceptance was everything I need. Tau's eyes saw me in raw form and was ok with who I am. He voiced his commitment to never attempting to change me. My honest words in a world of pretenders was music notes floating to his ears. He wanted to share his music with me. He disappeared and returned to the bathroom with a violin in his hand. Bengee had ran a bath for me but never bathe and serenade me. I closed my eyes and absorbed the sweet instrument dancing in my ears as my body inhaled the vapor in the air. He returned to side of the bathtub. I was relishing Tau's pampering. He mobilizes my body sponge. He grazed my neck down to my right shoulder with the soapy sponge. He swept the soapy sponge down my right arm beyond my elbow to my forearm. He caress my wrist, right hand, and between each finger with the soapy sponge. He individually washes each one of my fingers. He used his sex-pertise with the soapy sponge on my arm, elbow, forearm, wrist, hand and fingers on my left side. He squeezed the sponge over my chest. The soapy water cascaded down my breast and drips off my double chocolate nipples. The white soapy water on my sexy silky skin had harden his foreign chocolate. The soapy sponge applauded my fit abdomen and tenderly smooched my pussy. My lips released a slight moan of pleasure. My skin was unfamiliar with his genuine loving caresses but wel-cummed it. He lifted my right foot from the bubbly warm water. He washes my toes on my right foot one by one. The soapy sponge continues on the path of wanderlust pass my ankle to my calf, down my knee to my right thigh. He placed my washed right leg back into the bubbly water. He lifted my left leg out the bubbly water to rehash his sensual washing. To another person it just a bubble bath but the intimate convo

Saturday, July 29th

along with his Tau's heartfelt touch, it was more than what meets the eye. He shared his life travels from Africa to America. His pathway was something like Coming to America, minus the title and money, and he was 15yrs old looking for a music career and not a wife. I couldn't believe he never saw the movie. So we going to watch it now and then fuck. LMAO! BRB!

After feasting and feeling the exotic foreign chocolate for 3 hours per day for 2 day, my pussy was full but my mind was empty of confusion. I had one question for Naturel, and 2 people to confront. I needed to know Naturel's next move and I wanted to ask her in person. And I had to confront my feeling for Bengee and Earl. I decided to take Tau's advice and face Bengee and my feelings for him and stop trying to run from them. He also advised I do the same with Earl. I will consider it but now wasn't the time for Earl. Tau had stop by my brownstone by invitation around 11 in the morning and I sleep the rest of the day. I was worn out from him catering to my every move. Shit, if I had asked him to carry me to the bathroom it would've been done. LMAO! That foreign chocolate gets the best of me every time. LMAO! I got up at 5 am. I had to beat my face, lay my hair and calm my nerves. I couldn't wait to see what was in store on the tour. And on top of the jitters from anticipations of the meeting, my heart was beating sex-tra heavy for the dinner date with Bengee. Tau was my driver. His words of encouragement came with breakfast. It was the boost I needed. To walking into the 9 am meeting at 8:45 am with confidence in my step. My head and stomach full of myself. I ran into Tricky Nicky at the elevator. We complimented each other on each other shoes. This is the way Boss Bad Bitches,#triplebees, greet each other, acknowledging each other's status. She was killing a clementine orange sleeveless business cut dress with a pair of black open toed Jimmy Choo's. She walked me into the office room. There was a long desk with suits around the edges. Tricky Nicky introduced the suites. She started from the left side of the table. "This is Steven Greensburg the Accountant, he is responsible you're paycheck. I Tricky Nicky your Manager had booked you hosting. Some charity events, concerts, Emery's liquor debut at clubs, fashion shows which are all paid jigs. The paid jigs have signed contracts with Emery. The money is used to pay you and everybody in this room. Mr. Greensburg make sure that happens. I have commercial auditions and some media press time set up like guest appearances on radio and TV shows. This is all to build a name for yourself before announcing your relationship with Emery on Labor Day. Celebrities' life are planned out. Lime light relationship usually last about 3 to 4 months.

Yours and Emery's will last 4 months." She handed me the itinerary for my future. My eyes widen at the words:

August:

2nd Boston
3rd Albany
4th Philadelphia
5th Pittsburgh
6th Maryland
7th Washington
8th dinner with Emery/ Paparazzi will be in attendance
9th Oakland
12th San Francisco
13th San José
14th San Diego
16th dinner with Emery/ paparazzi will be in attendance.
17th Denver
18th Houston
19th Austin
20th Dallas
25th Minneapolis
26th Chicago
27th Detroit

Monday, July 31

28th Columbus
30th Raleigh

September 1st -3rd Hamptons/ relationship announcement

Holidays with Emery:
Halloween
Thanksgiving's Eve
Christmas's Eve
New Year's Eve
Valentine's Day
3/13 announcement of the break-up

You know Tricky Nicky once she started talking she didn't stop until she said everything on her mind. She continued "This is Vanessa Mickens Acting coach. You'll met with her every Monday at 5pm after your 3pm fitness training with Marcus. Sitting at the head of the table is the most Gifted and Talented man in the universe, Mr. Emery, the President of Emerald colored Diamonds (ECD) entertainment." Wow that was a hell of introduction but whatever. On the right side of the desk Tricky Nicky put names to Danni Casella my Personal Assistant, the Stylist that goes by just "Frenchie" and Walter, the photographer. "To change these words into fact all you have to do is sign these contracts, this contract is a gag order, meaning you are not allowed to talk about any of the employees here in this room, while in employed or if you're no longer working for the company. These contract is agreeing to a 10 thousand sign on bonus and 15 thousand per paid jig." I signed so fast the ink was still wet LMAO! After Mr. Greensburg handed me my check I had to start working. A 15 outfit photo shoot with Walter. Before I left the 6 hour photo shoot Tricky Nicky whispered in my ear I need a body guard, and I need to hire him myself. She suggested a "fuck-able" one since I was going to be on the road basically for the next 30 days. It was good advice, since she was clearly taking Emery of the table. LMAO! Nobody was checking for Emery. She could relax. I wonder what their relationship was like under the sheet, HUH! I had my phone in my hand to call Earl. Above it all he has been my friend that I share my life with. I had that Ivette feeling again. My phone vibrated in my hand. I received a text from Marcus, the chocolate gladiator, at 2:30pm with the meeting point but I had missed it. It was now 3 pm. I had 30 minutes to get to 91st street and 5 ave. I had to change in the back seat. Tau almost crashed cause he was taking peeks in the rear view mirror. LMAO! Marcus was a little tight off my lateness. No point intended. LOL! But I softened the bulging muscles in his neck with my great news of joining Emery's company. I posted a before and after pic of Marcus as my #MCM. His mad and happy face. LMAO! Both faces look the same. As we jogged around the Central Park's reservoir we ran through my future. Marcus had validated questions. "What are you going to "be" besides being Emery's Trophy for the world to see?" The question took me back to Will Smith's words written in stone. "Change the world!" I want to use my spotlight to shine on women like me and the ones that are not like me but had the thought of fucking a man or nicca real quick but never acted on it to not be ashamed of being whom they are. Why should women have to hide their sexual desire in fear of the labels "people" slap on the skin? Marcus also brought up the other question that was already floating around of Who would I hire as my body guard? The question rolled around in my head with the emotions about Bengee after I parted sweat and ways with Marcus. Tau drove me from the park to my brownstone and was on his way. He was adjusting well. He was learning how to hold his desire in my presence unless I flipped the on switch. LMAO! My stomach flipped around with anxiety. I was getting ready for dinner with Bengee. After curving Bengee for 15 days I had finally agreed to meeting up with him. By running from what I wanted I was chased into different beds pretending it was what I needed. I had to face Bengee eventually and I'm choosing now. I know I was wrong for spend unnecessary time with Bengee but I was hooked from his scent, his charisma, and his snake. The combination of the 3 puts my thinking in a trance of not working. But I couldn't be snagged. I genuinely enjoy our sex-periences. I definitely felt something for Bengee pass the skin and in my blood. So tonight's plan is to have dinner at my crib, yes up the stairs not in studio apartment. Yup I got my chef cooking with the pot on, AYE! Pasta with my homemade tomato sauce, cheese garlic bread and a healthy garden salad to start off with. I had bought 2 bottle of red wine. I had popped a molly and was sipping on one of the bottles. Maybe it was my nerves, the molly or the 90 degree weather but it is crying rivers on my forehead and between my legs. I had the flutters in my stomach and in pussy just off the thought of Bengee. I sat in the living room window like a bitch waiting on the mail man carrying her check. I watched him park his bright blue Lexus on the opposite side of the street from my brownstone under a street light. I could hear his boots chiming from the window and my pussy was listening. I ran to the front door my ears craved the live clicking of his boots. I didn't want to show him the thirsty is real, so I placed my ear up against the front door. I heard the boot's chimes grow from a faint to a booming beat. The thought of being skin to skin rolled in my mind and leaked between my legs. My pussy started pulsated so hard to beat of the chiming coming from his boot. It sounded like my pussy's lips was clapping. I was very happy to see him and my pussy was clapping and drooling like a toddler. I opened the door and came on myself. My knees prayed to serve him until the snake's eye tears anoint me with praises. I don't know what it is about a fresh hair cut that made a man's skin glow. Bengee's evenly spread dark chocolate skin glow from under the fresh cut lines around his waves in dark caesar. His money Mitch half-moon part slashed at my pussy and taste buds making me bleed salvia from my mouth and milk from my pussy. I want to go school daze on his ass and lick his curve on his head. LMAO! His euphoria cologne danced off his skin and put me in a trance. I thought about Bengee's snake over the 15 day but standing face to face with him I truly missed him the person over the snake. But as much as I wanted to tell him I missed him and want to plant kiss on his pretty brown eyes, large nose and juicy lips, I fought the yearning in my limbs and just grinned. He planted his lips over my lips. His tongue swam around in my mouth. He had kiss me before but today it felt like is heart was in his mouth and there was meaning to the movement. His tongue was comminuting love that couldn't be directly expressed. PYP wasn't flowing in my blood. PYP floating was absent in his blood as well. I had to pull away from his embrace I was drifting into an inappropriate state of fairy tale love. A world I don't live in. After the kiss that sucked the strength out of my knees, I started leading him up the stairs to the rooftop but we only made it to the 2nd floor. His boot's chiming as he walked up the stairs and his scent filling up the air sparked the beast in my taste buds. My taste buds took control and my thought flew out my mouth in a seductive whisper "I want to drink your babies." He feed my desires. My warm watery tongue outlined the snake's silhouette. I outlined the head, it's long neck and his 2 large shoulders. My taste buds could no longer take being taunted and my mouth ingested the snake's body. My lips tightly wrapped around the neck. Slowly I pulled my lips up from the shoulder to neck and the over the head of the snake. I gently drag my tongue around the meeting point of the head and the neck. I added salvia for lubrication. My hand glide up and down on the neck as my lips tended to the head. His hips lunged toward my face. The thrust filled with violent sexual force driving the snake to the back of my throat. I was neck and neck with the snake. I was mind fucking the head of the snake with my tongue while the body was in my mouth. My passionate wordless conversation with snake had creamy tears leaking from its eye. The snake planted his seeds on my taste buds. The flavorful seeds were filled with character, salty, sour and sweet. It was delicious and tasty. I had sucked the cream from his core. He weakly climbed the next set of steps to rooftop. I had lit 50 candles all around. The candle light glow under the moon's light made the sky dress up with sprinkling star cut diamonds. The open air scenery sex-cited Bengee's eyes. I served him the food I had prepared. We talked freely like we've done in the past. It was light never heavy words tossed in the air. Background stories where the best. He had walked through an adventurous life path with scars to prove it and still had a sense of humor when others would be carrying bitterness in bags from the journey. His mouth enjoyed the food and then feasted on my lips for desert. He peeled me out of my clothes like the skin off a banana. He tongued me down until I was on my back. My back press up against the plush pink L shape sofa and my chest against Bengee's skin was heaven I was floating on a pink cloud. His hand touched way past my skin and was stroking my emotions resting in my soul. His snake slithered into my rainy awaiting freshly groomed forest. It moved smoothly across the surface of my insides with a curve in its neck hitting the right spots. Sensation I didn't knew existed. Spots filled with warm emotional explosions of waves crashing down on the snake's body. Laying on my back with my feet in the air. He had one of my feet in each of his hands. His grip had my legs spread wide. He stood between my legs on his knees. He had fallen in love with me. I know from the way the snake was glided. Each stroke was just for me, he had dropped his heart into. I'm looking to the sky for the right words for my pussy to say, "I love you too but I love other dicks too "without exposing and hurting his feelings. The snake traveled deep to uncharted areas. His eyes stared through me. He was looking for love. My eyes didn't speak the words he was looking for. He flipped me from front to back. We were both standing. I was bent over the couch my face buried in the seat of the sofa, my moans and screams being suffocated. I was standing but my feet couldn't touch the ground. Touching the ground was like floating on the wave of emotions in his eyes, his touch and in the snake. My pussy was pulling against the streams of lust while my heart wandering into puddles of love. He was standing up right behind my fat ass. He parted my ass cheeks with his hands and pushed my ass up. As the snake crawled deep the neck dragged up and down my clit. A wave of sensation pulling from every part of my body crashed down on the snake. My lips cried wave's passion, coating the snake wave after wave. In each wave of creamy water it feels like I was drowning, my ears had popped. I could only hear sound at a distance. I heard love pending ahead. I was slowly drifting to the sounds. My mind pulled against the stream that flowed from my heart and my pussy. My mind considered the feelings on the horizon. My mind sense the times when weren't around each other, pussy paranoia getting the worse of his mind and my pussy's high anxiety getting the best of me by bodying niccas. I squatted on the couch, my ass in the air with my chest and face down. The snake strokes was repeatedly bursting into spots of creamy waves. My mouth wailed soft sounds of pleasure. My pussy wailed tears and loud moans from the pressure of the snake pushing my pussy's walls open. The tightness had squeeze words out of Bengee, he asked "how do I make this pussy mine?" His words ringed in my head like the metal hoops on his boots. The snake swam through my pussy, into my rectum and back in my pussy. The mixed creams and friction created truffle butter. The pleasure made my pussy slippery and my emotions slipped out my mouth. I said I love you out loud. It felt like it was going to be our last time fucking from the strokes of the snake. I know I couldn't let him back in pussy without opening my heart and mouth. It came down to him needing it or leaving it. Of course we fucked through the night and I fell asleep in his arms and woke up too fuck some more. But his question never stop waltzing around in my head as well as my confession. I have lease this pussy with option to buy but to hand over complete ownership was almost impossible. I can't leave my brownstone without everybody hollering at me and my pussy barking back. My pussy hustle got so many dicks, every dick pulling at me cause they hold some string that sews my pocket together. For all the dicks I've told I love it and the ones I don't love, it's too bad they don't know I really do love them all, in my own way for my own reason or season. They don't understand that there just so many of them. I feel bad I can't give each dick the proper attention and FUCK (Fun, Understanding, Caring, Kindness) they deserve for their money or for their pleasure, I just didn't have time for it. Bengee would be no different. I'm stuck here in between soaring into emotional bliss of the heart or sink into sexual fulfillment of my pussy. I don't know if I'm going to drown or fly. I wish I could make it easy to love me, but loving me is sharing me, and I know niccas don't like sharing their shit. It's hard to a find an Earl or Tau type that will take me as I am. I was willing to reach for love above the water filled with plenty seas of fish. But am I reaching over my head with my heart and not with my legs, to lands I couldn't see or find a way to, this place call love. A place I've never visited. My heart standing right in front of love's fire. Love changes people, places and things. Could love change me? I wiped the sweat off of his forehead from working my pussy. We were both chopped and screwed with emotion and sex-haustion. I love to play the pussy game but I'm willing to change how I play for Bengee. I wasn't sure what I meant by it but when I wrote it I was willing to make truth out of the words. He had to go to work. He didn't usually eat breakfast but this Tuesday morning my legs was going up. He left me hanging. He said he had to think about the future of our relationship. He was honest with his feeling for me. The feelings run pass the touch and he didn't know how to handle his touch not being the only feel to my skin. #respect! He made it look easy walking out the door after we had just fucked our emotions out into the open without looking back. I started packing my plane leaves in 24 hrs. AYE! To Boston. I'll be on the road for the next 7 days. I return to NY for just 2 day before going back on the road. Besides packing my luggage I was carrying question I needed answers to. Like what's really good with Naturel? Will I ever talk to Earl's ugly ass again? Will Bengee's heart accept me for me? Why is Emery going so hard for a fake relationship? He wasn't buttface ugly or dead broke, he could get a gurl or at least buy one. The one question I had to answer before I got to the airport was who was will I hire to be my body guard? I hate to say it but I can't take my notebook, remember how Tricky Nicky threaten to burn it last time? I'm locking this notebook in the safe with my bands in my room closet floor safe. Maybe I'll buy another notebook with a different cover and write down the drop. What do you think should I keep track of my sex-periences on the road? #thotyhotty your opinion. Right now I'm going to swing thru the hood check up on Mr. Buster and the grease monkey, BI as usually before I bounce TTYL! ☺

P.S I'll be checking the gram to see all the #thotyhotty post! LMAO!

www.ingramcontent.com/pod-product-compliance
Lightning Source LLC
Chambersburg PA
CBHW070053260626
47160CB00004B/1197